READ HERRINGS JOURNAL

# Read Herrings
## Literary Journal

*Printed by*

**READ HERRINGS**

*2008*

*First Edition*

## All Rights Reserved

This journal is copyright of
Daniel Scott Batten and Read Herrings
And any duplication of this journal
In all forms violates international
Copyright law. This journal reserves
One time rights to the works herein
And any additional editions
Of this very journal as the
Publisher desires so long
As it remains in this format.

Questions and Submissions
May be sent to:
Readherringsjournal@writeme.com

ISBN

978-0-6152-0235-8

# READ HRRINGS JOURNAL

*Is Edited by*

*Daniel Scott Batten*

*Cover Art By Amy Yampanis*
*See more of her work at*
*Artwanted.com/Amybatten*

*Dedicated to the Memory of:*

*A Fallen hero,*

*Jason McCune*

*(1984-2007)*

*and*

*Gardner Batten*

*(1924-2007)*

# CONTENTS:

POETRY

Pages 10-47

SHORT STORIES

Pages 48-63

POLITICS

Pages 63-73

PROSE/SATIRES/ESSAYS

Pages 73-83

PLAYS

Pages 83-120

# POETRY

# Thalassa

Thalassa, mistress of Neptune,
rolling liquid of moods,
Sea that frightens little feet,
and squeezes throats at high tide,
Sea that calls the young moon
in response to small desires,
Ocean grey, ocean green,
that spits on the past
in large angry waves,
throwing man and matter back
to shores of decay,
Troubled bodies immerse their pain
in waters at large
and wars become submerged
in maelstroms beyond science
where mystery remains
our chemistries are uncovered
and merge into the sea
of essential lymph
The primal home calls in magnetic waves
to becalm the plasma of universal fear
The rhythm of fluid energy caresses
the saline semen of neutrality.
rushes the viscous underbelly of tired souls,
in the saline serum of our return,
our blood, magnified
in homogenous minerality
Harmony, diluted in the currents
to the soft white sands of rest,
ever drawn to the shores by dreams,
we return to the sleep
of mother warm,
mother Thalassa

By Nadine Sellers

Art By Nadine Sellers

## Petition

Ah! Let us don the garb of pretense
let us be the model before the immoral
lending telegenic faces to the greatest cause
in the name of little intellect in the ready to wear
department of righteous indignation
after a fashion we seek facsimile
there assume nobility in signature
the right to litigate to mitigate
laudenum ad nauseum cum laude
we chose to agree we sign away
first in ink then in four color poster we frown
the public frown at private atrocities
first in ink then in water, tears come easily
to drown the public voice
the larger world the lesser cause
private interest public causes
the larger the populus the stranger vox populi
out of fashion out of favor
the word outrage becomes new rage
pen in hand the good suffer
this current affliction that pain du jour
another vehicle of fame and fortune
conductors of the vicarious wagon
find in the poet and the politician
the new antagonist of the next plot
to same place

By Nadine Sellers

## There's a little hobo in my heart who Forever gives the finger to humanity

for every time a father flips the dinner table
for every time a wife winds up at a motel
there's a little hobo in my heart who forever
gives the finger to humanity
for every time the cage door in solitary slams shut
for every time the police baton meets a bone
for every time a horse gets beaten in the stall
there's a little hobo in my heart who forever
gives the finger to humanity
for every time a family uses the stove to heat the room
for every time a teenaged soldier tries on a prosthetic limb
there's a little hobo in my heart who forever
gives the finger to humanity
for every time the sheriffs put still-warm furniture at the curb
for every time there's an ignored bedpan
there's a little hobo in my heart who forever
gives the finger to humanity
for every time something living is caught in the cross-hairs
for every time the warden signals for the IVs to begin dripping
for every time a father breaks his son
there's a little hobo in my heart who forever
gives the finger to humanity
for every time the outsider gets the shit kicked of them by the insider
for every time the repo man on stealthy heels arrives
for every time a city has to shut its lights & sound its sirens
there's a little hobo in my heart who forever gives the finger to
humanity
--

By Rob Plath

# Swarm

I feel the tremble

Trenchant waves leave my dormant state in ruins

You lie on good, vacant earth to call me forth

As leukocyte waves toss dirt from me

Destroying hate and longing

Contacting alabaster skin as I rise through you and linger

But for a moment to glare with eyes that tear through you

Seeing what outside forces have tried to warp

Make their own

Your refusal was nigh

Returning to this place and forcing yourself against the crust

To allow an exhausted mind, ill of amor fati

Clearance to see in speed not thought possible at you again

Strobing and piercing every piece, begging

Seduce from me ecstatic reveling

Blind me from the eyes of others here

Leave me no more

To await your corruption

By Aaron Foss

# Omvendt fjendebillede

Vi sad og var voldelige
slagtede hinanden med latteren gjaldende ud i rummet
Lod våbnene tale så blodet sprøjtede
med virtuelle stænk

jeg var kaptajn Sanders
og du mit billede af en fjende der ikke passede ind i verdensbilledet
vi udvekslede strategier
men holdt plottet for os selv

ingen tog det alvorligt
før metallet glimtede i vores øjnes eufori over de virkelighedstro lyde
og den smukke røde farve der kom
når kroppe blev malet op på væggene

vi troede det var festligt
og at de bagefter kom leende ud af rummene for at hylde os
men tavshedens knugende mønster
gav os tvivlen om vores handlingers afkom

nu fanger bordet
og gerningers grusomhed kræver altid en konsekvens
som da jeg skød hul i dit bryst
og blodets grafik forplantede sig

så længe det varede var det sjovt
bare ikke at opdage det sande væsen vi var blevet til
gennem legene der blev udpenslet
og forvredet til virtuelle spil

vi var uovervindelige helte
fejrede triumfer og hæder for gerninger der rakte langt ud over pligten
men nogen slukkede for vores virkelighed
og drev os ind i denne verden


tilbage til handlingernes konsekvens
og vores måder at takle
dens smerte på

## Reverse image of the enemy

We sat and was violent
Butchered each other with laughter resounding in the room
Let the weapons speak so the blood splashed
With virtual spatter

I was captain Sanders
And you my picture of an enemy who didn't fit in to the image of the world
We changed strategies
But kept the plot to ourselves

No one took it seriously
Before the metal flashed in our eyes' thrilled by the sounds' realism
And the beautiful red colour coming
When bodies were painted on the walls

We thought it was a joke
And they afterwards would come laughing out of the rooms to celebrate us
But the oppressing pattern of silence
Made us doubt the breed of our act

we are now caught
And the cruelty of actions demand always a consequence
Like when I shot a hole in your breast
And the blood was spread in graphics

As long as it lasted it was fun
Just not the discovery of the true being in which we were becoming
Through the play that became exaggerated
And twisted to virtual games

We were the untouchable heroes
Triumph and honour that reached far over the pledge was celebrated
But somebody switched off our reality
And drove us into this world


Back to the consequences of actions
And our way to handle
The pain

By *Tue Omø*

## MINDEBÆGER

På det lille blå morads af skygge
Ligger vi og gør op med det bestående
Mumler strofer fra gamle 60´er skiver
Gør dagens dont til nattens gerninger

Vi er drabanter i et cirkus på nedtur
Leger tigre og løver med domptøren
Slår smæld med pisken for ikke at tabe
Sender aben videre til den der tabte sidst

Er der en dag mere i betragterens glød
Eller har vi taget for givet at vi bare kunne blive ved
I sagens natur har vi overdrevet forførelsen
Men alt hvad der smager af liv vil mere

Men i aften er det forbi
Regnens trommen på din kind bekendtgør bruddet
Al lykke brænder ud
Og glæden dør

Men mindet vil altid være der

## MEMORY CUP

On the tiny blue piece of shades
We lay and talked against the existing
Murmuring pieces of songs from 60's singles
Doing a day's work to acts of the night

We are accomplished in a circus coming down
Playing tigers and lions with the animal tamer
Snaps the whip for not to loose sight
Pass on the monkey to the next in line

Is there a day more in the watchers ardour?
Or did we take it for given that we could go on
Naturally we have exaggerated the seduction
But all that tastes of life wants more

Tonight its over
The drums of rain on your cheek announce the break
All happiness fades away
The dying of joy

But the memory will always be there

By *Tue Omø*

## Perfekte illusioner

Man siger, at i morgen er der en bedre dag
Men hvis man vågner op til en regnvåd,
blæsende storm ind i øret
ærgrer vi os over håbet

Det siges at der altid er et lys i mørket
Men hvis ikke du selv tænder det, kommer du aldrig igennem
For det vil være opslugt
Indtil du tror på at lyset er der et sted

Det er blevet fortalt at lykken findes bag horisonten
Men hver gang du når den
Flytter den sig længere væk
Og pludselig står du i et fremmed land

Nogle tror på at livet er en illusion
Men hvis det er rigtigt, ville blomsten jeg snuser til
og farven jeg nyder
Være et sanseligt bedrag

Akkurat som vores tro på at der er en bedre dag, et lys i mørket eller lykken bag horisonten

Det eneste du kan tro på
Er at der er en ny dag
Og du er den eneste der kan give livet
det indhold du ønsker

Alt andet er en illusion…

## Perfect Illusions

You say that tomorrow is a better day
But if you wake up to rainy,
Blasting storm into the ear
You are annoyed over the hope

It is said that there always is a light in the darkness
But if you don't turn it on yourself, you'll never get through
For it will be absorbed
Until you believe the light is there somewhere

It has been spoken that happiness will be found in the horizon
But every time you reach it
The horizon has moved further away
And suddenly you are in a far away country

Some believe that life is an illusion
But if that's true, will the flower I smell
And the colour I enjoy
Be a sensuous delusion?

Precisely as in our belief in a better day, a light in the darkness or happiness in the horizon

The only things you can trust
Is that there will be a new day
And you are the only one to give life
The meaning you want

Everything else is an illusion…

By *Tue Omø*

# At the river

So easily found is hedonism,
Even more in whimsical youthful throes
And our money down depthless drains of throats!
Alcohol floats our boats down sea of haze
Then one faraway year, 'those were the days'


I felt like a walking human cliché,
                *As hungover as a debauched sailor*
My temple throbbing, (I thank you booze Gods)
Among the knoll of the seagulls' rabble
I stared at the mirthful rivers' babble


Daffodils spectated from the bank as
Loverless boats bobbed gently to lute breeze
Willows wept, mourning the passing of Spring
On the fierce rapids a heron strutted,
Protagonist in a beauty tableau

The effervescent orb then ascended
Coaxing a birdsong concert, basking all.
Smoke trails latticed Cerulean sky
And whilst gazing at this giant mural
I thought of the pricks in bed addled still
 And it almost induced me to spew up


*By* Jonathan Doherty

## untitled

Luscious cauchemar ostentatious comme suite,
The lotus et lost sheep,
And a coup de traître ravishing contentment (contention)
Into an eye-sore, then extinct.

Et Amoré? Love = Adore: adoré
Jé rêve of she,

With those enombrable eyes
Diluted in LA beauté du diable,
Et lips as rouge as a rose!

Hors d'haleine with the sol se tourner
Et se retourner above the
Virgin day.

Caractéristique of Sunday
A beautiful day à la cherche,
A belle morn in the sun
As a ladybug flaps its wings
Landing gently on red lips
Pursed lovely with desire,
A kiss.


BY Aaron Howell

## The whispering from the wall

The wall just stood there looking boring and grey
But if you listened closely
You could hear the wall whisper
"Paint on me"

Something like wonderful paintings and greetings
Or funny drawings for a laugh
And the wall whispered
"I want more"

But one day something else was made
A little boy said it looked like a giant spider
So the wall whispered
"Erase me"

Days went by and the spider was still there
The boy's mother told him it was an evil sign, called swastika
And the wall whispered
"Tear me down"

Suddenly an early morning men came standing and looking
They erased all the evil drawn there
The wall whispered
"A 100 thanks"


By Lene Skovsende

## *What became of the hurting?*

I knew it very well
You were ageing
But still very stubborn
You were able to do so much
And I wondered

But one day they called
You were getting week
Sickness had you broken
given up living
one day together we had

It happened so quickly
They called me once again
I heard it but continued
The tears were waiting in the corners
I lost my father and best friend

But what became of the tears?



By Lene Skovsende

## Sorrow ship

Silently he's sleeping
Into the long night
Passing through the gates that leads to
Fairy shores so bright

First to set for sunset
The daughter of his smile
Waiting for the tide to say
Goodbye for a long while

Sailor you lost direction
When home was destination
And the heart clinging to life

Childhood memories
Coming by looking in his eyes
Old man sailor has set the course
To find his paradise

By Lene Skovsende

## The forgotten child

He wasn't found on the scanner
Only 2 was in sight
They were sewing the mother back together
When they felt another life
A boy, a tiny little boy

He came in the incubator fighting for his life
The 2 others were cute
When they were heading home, one was missing
The nurse came hastily
With the tiny little boy

3 was really an unlucky number
For his bed stood on the other side of the room
Even when they were sitting by the table, he was at the end
When they walked the streets, he was behind
The quiet boy

In school he was never asked
His brother did
At birthdays and Christmas, he was the last to get presents
The friends ignored him
For he was the tiny

When they moved from home into a common apartment
He had to be in the living room, there were only 2 rooms
Even the fancy door sign could only show 2 names
His name were written on a homemade cardboard sign
He didn't contradict

They bought a common car, a Mercedes
He only saw it from the backseat
Loving the holidays in Florida, especially air travel
For they could sit together
And he smiled

There was something he loved
Working in the record store
But the success lasted a short while
They had to fire an employee
There was no room for him

Though one cared for him
The parrot, Jacob, they all shared
Even when he was rejected jobs all the time
And forgot about everything, him self too

2 years went by with short lasting jobs
Without finding the right path
His brothers and sisters shared a designer company
He decided to be alone for ever
The boy became a man

He said goodbye to Jacob
Packed his belongings in boxes
Left the apartment without looking back
Standing on the platform waiting for the train
For ever taking him about

Who was he?

*The forgotten child!*


By Lene Skovsende

# IMPRESSION

Impression is stylized compression
An acquisition twice folded
And neatly
    Warmed by principal heat
    The curious phenomenon
        Gone
    And replaced by conformed
    Con ception
      A qualified deception:
    Erection
    Titled too far to the left
    To stand but briefly
    Concrete.

Impression is stylized compression
An acquisition twice folded
And neatly
    Warmed by principal heat
    The curious phenomenon
        Gone
    And replaced by conformed
    Con ception
      A qualified deception:
    Erection
    Titled too far to the left
    To stand but briefly
    Concrete.

By Daniel Scott Batten

## HARVEST MOON ON 9/21

Last night's moon was a round basket of golden grain
With a dark rim of intertwined twigs...
It was a wooden bucket left swimming
Upon the well's bright blue circle...

Last night's moon was a chalice
Of molten gold, of liquid stars...

It kept me up for hours,
The window blinds, although tightly shut
Still glowed with a pale blue fire,
Which was seeping through
And dropped its fluid light
Upon my closed eyelids, that
Like the window blinds,
Were unable to keep it out...

It wasn't just a moon last night,
But magic pot of liquid gold,
Being emptied into my thirsty soul
To ease its loneliness past midnight...

BY RITA ANDREEVA

## Harvest Cycle

i paint dreams in paisley
look how they made me stroke
complex tears across the fabric
of forested thought
enriched textures that pass
through finger tips
exciting lips to read minds
with recitation
this is the resuscitation of memories

remember these nights
inked in indigo
the tender dialog of trumpet flows
searching for an ear
to flood with secrets temptation
and the reminiscence of change
cascading into brimmed hats
weighing heavy on your mind

tonite i wear the disguise of myself
as an unmarked constellation
connected only by the science of imagination
arms outstretched to reach all corners
of the U.N.I.
spread your wings in the night dear children
we are all due to fly

By Shawn Terri

## By Sun And White Iron Moon

I've driven long and hard
with thirst to impure lips
and sand in hungry teeth
crossed the desert with hell skies
and giant cement rocks
quartz on eyelids
I've slept under somber drapes
of fear without reason
in the animal night
I've drank the blood of the hare
with the long black legs
hidden in the sage
I've stalked the evening coyote
raw nerve and red eye
on his primal path
swollen lungs and dry breath
ran the scorching sands
where the rattler awaits

and when I met the crow
dragging my shredded past
by sun and white iron moon
I dug a warm river
Where no one could follow.

By Nadine Sellers

## moustaches of death

when i was ten years-old
i used to like playing in
the woods nearby
my neighbor chris and i
spent hours wandering
through paths
once we found this tree
with a giant white cocoon
in it
we got closer and saw that
it was filled with black
caterpillars
it disgusted us
this squirming sack
insects were enemies
to us back then
we liked to torture
and kill all bugs
like bored, warped
princes of the woods
so we took sticks
and began to beat
this piñata
filled with creeping
dark moustaches
it broke open finally
and we whacked it harder
green jelly oozed from
their bodies
we kept swinging
white threads of the cocoon
stuck to the tips of our sticks
along with green guts
& little black hairs
when we finally were through
we had destroyed the womb
in the vee of the tree
a few filaments still clung
to the bark
we tossed our sticks
and walked up the path
fulfilled enough
to return to our homes

By Rob Plath

## AN IRAQI SOLDIER'S DREAM
## (for Jason)

He is infected
by a mosquito's pinching probe,
threading through veins
stinging his dreams.

First night in the desert, he
slept well.
He awoke in front of a
luscious swimming pool,
drinks served, chairs neatly placed
side by side,
he plunges in.
Floating around on his back,
the sky breaks into dots
from the leavened sun.

The boom and shatter grow louder;
foreigners make their way hurriedly
soldiers pass by in tanks as
buildings erupt in every direction.
The blitzkrieg burst of machine guns
stop many in their tracks,
some are tossed like dolls
in front of the rolling thunder on wheels,
their blood leaving trails in the dirt.

*Everyone becomes the enemy*,
he's not reassured by this statement.

Some spring into alley ways,
preferring the possibility of death by collapsing architecture
than flesh wounds ripped by streaming bullets.
Others hail a taxi
like it is any other day,

no fear of sabotage.
The village holds everything they've ever had
and have no intention of giving it up.

The fighting stumbles finally to fatigue,
but the dream will continue on
letting loose to infect the world again.

By Joseph Veronneau

## HIDDEN AMONGST THE TAMARACK

Who lives in those houses?
The ones you see from the road

with their many junked cars
and cracked satellite dishes

and ancient collapsed outbuildings
gathering moss and dust?

Sometimes you can catch a glimpse
of laundry billowing from a post

or the unevenly attached
trailer home as a shed or porch

with ill-matching lawn chairs
and life's debris strewn all about.

Their long dirt chained driveways
and loud "No Tresspassing" signs

make one always wonder,
"Who would want to go there?"

by

Roy C. Booth

## DRY RED SWEET WHITE

First Merlot –
Second blush –
Finish me
Off
Captain
With some white!
This
Is the
Woe
Of sailors
Toil:
By lantern,
By
Cape Cod Light,
We sail
Toward
Insanity
Tonight.

By Daniel Scott Batten

Sailing Off Cape Cod while sailing
Aboard *Bay Lady II*

# A Hole

Lately, I am acutely aware of the hole-dead center-
that hurts when a careless breeze whistles inaudibly through it.
I cannot remember a time when I was without it.
I once thought (and often still do) to fill it with jazz,
cigarettes, old photos, etc.
For a time, this treatment was successful enough so that at least I could forget about it briefly.

I once was optimistic in the hopes that another might fill it.
This was an attempt to deny responsibility.

I do not remember creating it.
It was just there and seemed as though it had always been.
I tried filling it in with memories but that only kept me awake all night.
Music and a few charmed books soothe it for intervals.
Belief helps, I suppose, but not entirely and again, never for long.
I think I have witnessed others experiencing it although i am not certain.
It feels like mine.

-Kevin M. Hibshman

# FĚÅħ

Hoesh dayĕ baoshmôrax
Oeīånåtn. Dalä-rshlåsht
Veomôr ageīshmôrshīt of
Shushrxā ħovħohī oatdayĕmôr
Shmôrahĕmôrīsħ forshtī
Whshrsh ĕll agebaårđt
Oatshushrx ĕdrsh of låfsh
Dayrvth wåħ ĕteårĕtåomôr –
Fĕåħ dayto sttx, sttx ĕt
Ldcåmôrħeh ĕt agetånelåaåīx
Of ĕ tåmôrħehlsh lstĕr oatbax
Ageeolåax of nshrsh đotårsh
Wållålā tdc đosåeshr
Oatåmôrīvåīushlx cmôrow
Äħageearsåsħ of ħ shzåtīt
Amor åī; äħageđoħehnĕ of
Shushrx ĕton donĕrcsħ åī,
Ĕt hĕt äħrsīoħehmôråysħ
Oatāgĕētont basīonsh wåtsh
Dalĕtont, oatĕtdayĕ aollsīīåush
Äħtestct eshrnĕmôrshmôrash.

## FAITH

Hope is a bouncy
Optimism. It relies upon
The tenets of our every
Thought and is an enchanted
Forest where all the birds
And every acre of life is
Rush with aspiration –
Faith is so easy, easy as
Looking at the simplicity
Of a single leaf and by the
Policy of mere desire you
Will soon look deeper and
Intuitively know that the
Creed of God exists in it;
That the dogma of every
Atom has marked it, as has
It recognized you and then
Atoms become wise to
Atoms, and this is a collective
That speaks permanence.

By Låīīlsh Shnbashr

# V.

Liquēre, licour
For the soul,
Be ice, take this
Advice and
Līquī-fy.

(Be liquid, liquor,
for the soul,
Be ice, take this
Advice and
Melt)

By Daniel Scott Batten

## the gladiators

long before i began writing
the typewriter made my gut jump

in a good way that is

the entire machine intrigued me
from the keys to those two thin
metal rabbit ears in back
that held the paper up

same goes for liquor bottles
long before i ever cracked a seal
the different colored bottles
set something off in me

i sensed something
good & powerful in these things
& then a few years later
i found i was right

they are the true weapons
of gladiators

By Rob Plath

# **C**ATHARSIS

Counting syllables to a tear like tap
Which soundtracks my rhythmatic ennui
yelled "Escape the painful tedium! "

New York aspirations of Northern town,
Heaved under a chrome sky, sun gold gilded.
Lost in architectural canyons,
Another day pushing sadness to margins

My ragged Vicious tee shouted; Rebel
To deaf ears of adhesive young couples,
My Dean turn-ups and Moz quiff ignored by
Lads with 'I drink therefore I am' mantras

Down Granada way the factories shut,
The uniformed workforce march transportward
To suburban lives, pubs, cul-de-sac chats
Tabby cats, the jigsawed postcode mural

A Harry's later I watch Irwell's blood,
Its liquid plasma, drift to the Quays and
Dusk forms an gritty ocular photo,
Another for my minds' battered scrapbook

Salford stands, an Angular Picasso,
Printed against a post-Lowry backdrop
The acoustic rush of the Met echoes,
Drowns Castlefield's vacuum of silence

Easily life is not too bad
I'm relishing the trudge back to Chorlton
 To Glenn Miller and a special chow mein

 By Jonathan Doherty

## **At the river**

So easily found is hedonism,
Even more in whimsical youthful throes
And our money down depthless drains of throats!
Alcohol floats our boats down sea of haze
Then one faraway year, 'those were the days'

I felt like a walking human cliché,
As hungover as a debauched sailor
My temple throbbing, (I thank you booze Gods)
Among the knoll of the seagulls' rabble
I stared at the mirthful rivers' babble

Daffodils spectated from the bank as
Loverless boats bobbed gently to lute breeze
Willows wept, mourning the passing of Spring
On the fierce rapids a heron strutted,
Protagonist in a beauty tableau

The effervescent orb then ascended
Coaxing a birdsong concert, basking all.
Smoke trails latticed Cerulean sky
And whilst gazing at this giant mural
I thought of the pricks in bed addled still
 And it almost induced me to spew up

By Jonathan Doherty

## Pretentious, *Moi*?

Sometimes a writer
Is accused of pretension.
But the allegation
Is frequently unfair.
To write that way
Is to scribble
Dishonesty.
While
Words from the heart,
No matter how
Flowery,
Are never
Pretentious.

By Mark Cantrell

# **UNTITLED**

Retire your mind
Speak nothing of forgotten lessons
Learn from me a rebel yell
In sarcastic dialect
That will fall only on the ears of
Poets
Paupers
Playwrights
Wheelmen
The future minds of those who determine legacy
While I grant amnesty to your being
Willing you into peace


By Aaron Foss

## Ill-Fated

Oh, the plans. The discord, the people
that influence such conclusions.
Disorder, face to face.
How to avoid disaster and destruction.
Exchanging our mutual despair
set to the musings of hard rock music.
Together, we come up with
a new disease, well-suited
and tailored for our particular woes.
The happiness around us an aberration,
people pretending enthusiasms
over coffee, ice cream, whatever
delicacy fits.

But we don't want an evolution:
satisfaction is obtained
sulking on this breezy landscape
of grass, dogs chasing tennis balls
from energetic owners,
people embracing in happiness.
See, we don't need all of that.
But, the embracing doesn't sound that bad,
a little love never hurt anyone
nor does lust, right?
Isn't this the part where
we are suppose to fall for each other,
pulling on the edges of each other's shirts
for more? You putting your hand
where things become stiff,
me running my hand over your
begging ample breasts?

Rather than becoming this
cherished illusion,
let us continue on
towards an afternoon of dimming down
our pasts,
and coloring our futures
in the correct grey.

By Joseph Veronneau

# *SHORT STORIES*

# Apeman in the City

Greg Fallon

Male prostitution was never an easy profession.

Frank sighed at this thought. The smell of the city right after it rained made it difficult to concentrate, a thick concoction of ozone, smog, and filth. To add to the atmosphere, the ground was covered by wet, rifled papers thrown away by their past owners. Dingy, dank, it would disgust some, but for Frank there was something comfortable about it.

His cigarette was almost out, taking one last puff; he dropped it to mingle with the trash all around. The orange glow blazed, but after a short amount of contact, it fizzled and was indistinguishable from the rest of the debris. Stepping out from the opening of the alley, he made his way into the stream of people heading to a nearby bar, a place known to have customers.

Hands in his pocket, he squeezed his fists, half because of the cold, and half because of the emptiness. No money, no cigarettes, not even chewing gum; he hadn't had a job or home in nearly three months. Being destitute can have a way of making your morals very flexible, and so, here he was, sinking to the oldest profession known. In junior high, this was considered an ideal job, something all the boys in his class had hoped to be. However, in reality, that concept had lost its luster; beautiful women find paying for companionship very unattractive, in fact unbeknownst to junior high boys, most women find it unattractive.

This brings us to the concept unfathomed by junior high children.

Who would pay? As the thought approached him, so did the destined establishment.

Across a congested intersection sat a modest brick building, with deep green overhangs and windows darkened to restrict people from seeing in. It should be noted that in appearance, there was nothing sinister about the building, but the feeling inside Frank's empty stomach made it feel as if he were entering hell. Carefully, he melded with others crossing the street, knowing full well the sobering experience he would undertake was making it impossible to concentrate on the oncoming traffic.

That task achieved, he paused. Last chance. He turned back expecting everyone to be watching this last step from a chasm edge. Reaching, not looking, as if to cushion the act, he found the handle for the door, pulled and walked in.

A quiet, jazzy music floated up to create atmosphere, lingering with barely audible voices. The place was dim, with just enough light to see the path to the bar, which gleamed like a beacon. Each step he took so slowly, feeling his feet sink into the plush carpet. What he wouldn't have given to lie down on that floor for a few hours, just one more dream.

Easing onto a stool, he kept his head looking down, using only his eyes to look around. The bartender made his way over, a tall, lanky man with a moustache asking the inevitable question, "What can I do for you?"

"Just a water."

The only response this got was a dirty look, as the bartender proceeded to get the glass, he spoke again, "Even the water isn't free here, son."

"Then don't bother, I haven't got a dime. But since you're here, maybe you can help," The words left Frank's dry throat, but seemed to be coming from somewhere else, "I need money, I'll do anything. Know anyone who can help?"

This produced a small laugh in the somber man, "Yeah. Thought that's why you're here. Give me a second, I'll send him to you."

With this the bartender retreated to the other side of the bar, proceeded to lift the bar gate, and walked into the darkness. A moment later, he returned and went back to the bar, proceeding to fix a drink. He then brought it to Frank, flashed a smile and said, "Compliments of a friend, better drink up. He'll be right over." Then as if they had never spoken, the man stood back, turned and continued wiping a glass absent-mindedly with his dishtowel. Frank obliged the man by finishing the drink in a mere minute, exhaling loudly.

The carpet of the area gave way to tiles when it was a few feet of the bar, giving Frank warning someone approached from the click of shoes behind him. As he went to turn, a thick hand rested on his shoulder. There stood a contradiction of a man: large and obese, yet seemingly humble, wearing a small pair of glasses as if to parody his girth. He squinted at Frank and gave a shy smile through a neatly trimmed beard.

The man's name was Chris, and apparently he was not new to the situation, wasting no time to lead Frank less than a block away, where there sat a rather mediocre inn. The man at the desk looked up very briefly from a copy of 'Papillion' and waved him through, not even handing him a key, suggesting that Chris had been planning this. Finally arriving on their floor, he was led to a very plain appearing door with the marking '3F' written on a piece of masking tape. Hastily digging out the key, Chris ripped open the door, the action accentuated by his heavy breathing.

Once inside, the door locked, he nervously plodded over to the bed and kicked his shoes off. Sitting down, he hunched over, sighed loudly, and looked up at Frank.

"You're perfect, perfect size." As he spoke, Frank couldn't help but notice his bizarre hand gestures as if communicating with a deaf man. "So how much will I be paying? I like strange stuff, I don't mind paying more." He then beamed, and as he did, his face shook and began to shine with perspiration. Frank smiled, trying not to betray his fear of the situation, "I don't mind strange, in fact, it's starting to be what I expect these days." His voice trailed off as the sentence ended, while he looked around at his surroundings trying to relax. It was then his voice seemed to take over for where his mind stopped, "200 dollars." This was more than he needed, he would have done anything for fifty. To his surprise, Chris agreed, telling him to go in the bathroom, wash up a little, and put on the outfit next to the sink.

Now inside the small, poorly lit bathroom, the 'outfit' consisted of nothing but a fake leopard skin loincloth, but for 200 dollars this was little to object over. Finished changing, he stepped out and turned, to smile, his tongue placed firmly between his teeth to keep from laughing out loud. There stood Chris wearing a sailor suit of white and green, complete with hat and kerchief around the neck. The suit was a size too small making a few obvious bulges, something Frank was trying not to look at. It was some kind of disturbing 'doughboy' visual, and it wasn't pretty.

Impatiently, Chris motioned him to approach, instructing him to lie down on the bed and close his eyes. Frank tried to imagine the beach, or something comfortable and safe as he felt Chris' hand on his knee. But as much as he tried the image of Chris as a sailor kept creeping back. Terrifying.

Then things went wrong.

Suddenly, a pillow was being pressed hard against his face, as all of Chris' girth was upon him. He tried desperately to hit Chris' arm, to tell him to stop, but it became clear that Chris had no intention of stopping. The pillow pressed harder to the point where it felt his nose would break, and his arm flailed to grab something. He could feel the smooth surface of the night table, and grabbed something on it with the palm of his hand. He then swung wildly where he believed Chris' head to be, and after two tries made contact, and felt Chris tumble off him.

Frank rolled off the other side of the bed, breathing wildly, and pulled himself up, his back to the far wall in the room. Chris stood on the other side of the bed, glasses and hat disheveled, still holding the pillow. At this point, Frank glanced to see what he had used to hit Chris, and saw he was holding a black phallic object, reacting with a small scream, he dropped Chris' 'friend.' Looking back at his antagonist, "What are you doing, man? What is this?"

"I'm sorry, I don't have 200 dollars I can spend. I have a wife… kids… besides, I did say what I wanted was a bit strange." Chris gave another of his seemingly harmless grins.

With speed not normal for a man of his size Chris bolted over the bed after him, Frank, screaming, as he ran away. After running around the room a few times, Frank grabbed the lamp and pulled as he ran, unplugging it and making the whole room pitch black. Everything went silent for a minute, Frank inching towards where he sensed the door would be. He could hear Chris, moving like a dinosaur, his weight equivalent, to put the lamp back on. Suddenly an idea entered his head; he started to stalk the sound, like a lion stalking his portly prey, judging that Chris would be turned away to plug the lamp back in.

And there was light. As predicted, Chris' size would require time equal to the earth in order to turn on his axis (roughly 24 hours), and Frank pounced, landing right on his back. He held tightly to Chris' ridiculous kerchief, reminding him of Captain Ahab and Moby Dick. The world flew around him as Chris spun, repeatedly backing into walls, then, finally Chris fell, to his knees first, and then on to his left side, making gargantuan gurgling sounds as he did. Turning the behemoth on his back, he didn't need a medical examiner, Chris' wife and kids had lost their cow.

Like an animal incensed, Frank rushed to the desk looking for Chris' wallet, and found the leather bound article in his cast aside pants. Inside were six crisp 20-dollar bills, not equivalent to 200, but would this suffice for the pain and labor? As he made for the bathroom to get his clothes, a knock at the door and a voice, "Could you please open the door, sir?" It wasn't a question, and judging from the size of Chris, Frank would be charged with killing about three people, maybe more.

Stuffing the money in his loincloth, careful not to get any paper cuts, Frank made his way to the window, and pulled back the shades. It couldn't be opened, so he picked up a chair and smashed it, after the second hit, the sound could be heard in stereo as the inn manager pounded on the door. The window gave first. He stuck his head out to see if there was a ledge, and seeing none, he looked to the only type of support: a cable that ran up the side of the building.

He eased out, careful to avoid any broken glass, and took the cable in both hands. With a swing, he tried to slide down, but the staples gave way first, and he screamed as the cable let go from the building. As he fell down, one staple apparently held, and his fall turned into a glide, heading right into the crowd of people walking on the sidewalk. Amid shouts of, "It's Tarzan!" Frank crashed into a businessman on his cell phone, hurting his back slightly.

He stood but could only hunch over from his back, and tried to tell everyone to remain calm, but could only mouth vowel sounds with all the adrenaline pumping. With no one to understand him, and people calling him 'Apeman,' he became infuriated, yelling and shaking his fists. This having no effect, except for some tourists who seemed to take an endless amount of pictures, he galloped off around a small child and her scared mother, through the crowd and to safety, 120 dollars safely in his crotch.

Picture for HISTORY OF A SPECK

And is Drawn by Greg Fallon

# THE HISTORY OF A SPECK

I arose from a panic and stood outside looking at the skyline, the wind laughing as it whipped my hair and my soul into a flurry of *feelings*. Sentiment whirled furiously in me, my body tingled with *life* and my eyes saw the blur of yesterday turn into a nebulous stretch of omnivorous sky. My arm dangled arduously at my side, and when I attempted to lift it in an attempt to move the hair from my face, it spoke *defiance*. It *cackled* at my *insubstantiality*. I soon realized that I was alone; I woke up outside facing the brutality of self, the sheer terror of loss, the ugliness of regret.

A distant sound caught my ears and in it was music, the bewitching plunk of keys that sounded like her jazzed up version of Beethoven's *Moonlight Sonata.* I leaned upon the steel railing desperate to see her – to see her walking, her brown hair trickling behind her, her sexy hips swaggering *voluptuousness*. It did not matter; the more I looked at the streets, the more real it became that she was gone. I would never experience her again; the way she smelled, the way her eye twitched when she was nervous. When she was in the car or out at one of the pubs with me, her hand would shake when she was inspired to play. She is, or rather, she was.

My hands loosened and fell limp at my side and I fell back until I rested on the wall of my apartment. The music faded and I reflected upon what her mother used to say, "Everyone can be a writer, so what is so special about you?" Of course, I was polite, and I didn't entertain her with some angered repose. I just smiled at her wretchedness and looked upon the serene lips of her daughter whom I so dearly loved. Yes, it is true, everyone says they are a writer and they treat words like words owe them meaning. They speak and make use of words like love as if love owed it to the pen to be **bold** and responsive when it is us who owe everything to love. Love owes us nothing. We do not deserve love, and yet we put expectation on it thinking that meaning is a *definition*. We owe words too. We owe it to them to have meaning so they can inspire, move, and tear down kingdoms as well as build them up. Oh my dear and sorry world, who in desperation, make love as petty as they make their lives. Live I say! Live and one day you will be in exaltation! You shall look to the stars and not see stars, the day when you look upon space and not see time! This is life! Arise all you dead souls! Arise. Yet, in this instance, I was preaching more to myself then to the world that rejected *writers* and their words. I was he that begged *why?* I was the definition, I was the metaphorical *ambiguity* that looked nice but missed the right *experience*. My *poetry* sounded more like misery, it had a voice that appalled me, and worse, it made me sick to be a writer. I wished I had never known passion, passion being the very morsel of her that I found most astounding. I found her astounding. She, she, well she destroyed words. She blasted away all that I *knew* with her desire to wonder.

My soul curled up into a shriveled mess as I yearned to be sitting, gazing, and longing to see her sitting in her seat sipping her black coffee, cigarette raging with brutish scandal of tragic twirl. Her eyes *composing*, indicting stillness to *speak* to her in notes, she made music from my theories that I shared with her. She stirred wild fires from my insane love of the obscure. She drank from my soul to feed her inner lust for *sound*. She gave me her ears. Wait, no! She gave me her soul when I read out loud my poems she heard each vowel as separate strings pulling the varying *sensitivities* of her inner piano. You see, she carried her piano inside her. She was her piano; she loved that piano more then me, more than God. Well, at least I imagined her to hear me in that way. Everything was better when she was around. Tuna fish tasted like ambrosia, coffee tasted sweeter, crackers might as well have been tenderloin. She was my food, my nourishment. She gave me love and she gave me infinity. I learned that anything precious was to be worshipped by that smallness inside of us. She used to take me on night hikes up Mount Monadnock so I could see the limits of our world. She loved the *music* played in the stars. She heard it, and she tried to make me hear it too. I did not; I only heard my body sing for her. Sing to hold her close, to kiss her, to hear her heart beat as we lay on a blanket with my head on her chest, as she taught me the constellations once more.

    She would always carry with her a small round magnifying glass that she would raise up to the sky to see the detail, to witness each *particular*, each sweeping hand of color, each *tentacle of light*. She would *brave me* to look, to see beyond the dot of distant illumination. She implored me to see the grandeur that oozes from such alien reaches of time. She would sparkle, her entire body seemed to levitate and her aura would be crisp and bright. She would tell me her theories on time travel, how by looking at each star we are engaging ourselves in the past. We are looking upon the fantastic essence of millions and maybe even billions of years of light, which she would call, *God's Face.* Her theories grew each time we climbed Monadnock, each time getting increasingly complex. I would listen in silence, overjoyed by her titanic *feel* for God. She described how all things came from a tiny speck in the sky that heated up, burst, and from this burst came the elements of life. She then would speak of the spectacular unlikelihood of life evolving on earth, not to mention, anywhere. She knew as much about Einstein as she did about Whiten. It is, *where she got her knowledge of music;* and she is where I got my knowledge of poetry. She filled my glass; she mistreated me with too much richness of being. The acquaintance, the mere essence of her stirred in me the alchemical gold of expression. When she was away on trips and tours for her piano playing, I knew when she was going to arrive home. I would smell her, dream of her and that is the day she would come home. I always knew, and she always tried to surprise me. She was so, wildly sexy, so, *tangible*, so extraordinarily *substantial*. She drew me with lines, with sensitivity, with her tenderness, her feel for what was true, or at least true in me. She would arrive and what lie dead inside me resurrected with new life. She was spirituality, she was grace, and she was everything perusable and everything indefinite. She blessed me with totality.

    Sirens drove by and I was once again brought back to the truth of her absence. My ears screamed and my head burned, my very nature crawled with despair. I clenched my fists tight until blood spilled from my hands. I Bit my lip and felt warmth fill my mouth. I fell to the ground, curled up in an awkward pile of self, and wept, sharp pains shooting up and down my torso. I turned cold and clammy, my eyes hurt so truly they wished to explode from their sockets. I just sat there, feeling the Northeastern air blast me into a catatonic stasis. I felt like an open wound, like I was an injury about to pour out my lifeblood.

In my hysteria, I started to mumble to her, calling her name and asking her to play something by Chopin. I remember this because I was lucid, yet I could she her sitting at the piano, I could see her vying the piano to speak to her – so I wanted to feel her play one more song. She leaned in to play and that is when she disappeared on me again. I felt her loss now, I felt the last ember of hope deflate, all that held me up, crashed, and I was loudly aware, that I was *solitary*. Just as quickly as I realized my situation, my senses shut down and I began to reflect upon her. How she would sit for hours drinking whiskey sours, arousing the keys to voice her every desire. Fire rose from her when she played, I could feel her emotions as they burned from the glory of her playing. She lived and died by the texture of each note, the smoothness of each transition. She etched into the air goodness, she gave vitality where lay void. Her hands were so *polysyllabic*, so elegant and versed in mood and *behavior* she commanded the audience to feel whatever she desired. She made love to the piano, she wrapped herself around each vibration and I was so intoxicated by the experience, I too was driven to sensual planes unknown and unfelt by man and his limited rapture. Just as soon as she was driven to climax, my pen spilled its ink upon the page and spoke her *eminence*. Each word glistened with her *majesty*. I felt refreshed, she felt, no she exuded; release and rebirth. She died and came back to life with each piece. She put herself upon the cross and sacrificed herself for each one of us, so we may know God. *God lives in between the notes*, she would say, *God is the full richness of the exponential experience of the music, the mood and the resulting emotions.*

As she laid upon the piano regaining her strength, I would walk up to her, whisper in her ear, *you are the brightest of all stars*. One day, the day before she died, she replied to it, *yes but stars are the brightest before they wane and burn out*. I was awestruck by this, but I did not see the coming *anticipation*. She smiled and masked any pain that might have been welling up inside. She put her hand on my cheek, and said *I was worth more to her than all the specks and all the notes in the world. I love you,* she dripped with a species of marvel that pronounced itself with such unbridled affection, *and you are the soul that gives me all this vitality.* I melted, her powers where so encompassing, so entire, I could feel my soul liquidate and pour itself into her. She sipped me so regularly and I could *taste* her feelings.

She turned to me at lunch, as we sat in a local café on Canal street in downtown Manchester, and told of this dream: *I was on a ship alone. It was calm but the sky was mad with storm, and its insanity made me feel free. I felt a slight breeze and in a whisper came the words, eundo et reduendo[i] (going and returning).* She paused, sipped her cigarette, sighed and putting her hands in mine, she continued, *I looked upon the moon that rose from the horizon, and it turned to show a face, and it smiled at me and said, 'et sic ad judicium (and so to judgment).'*

After this we drove to the Manchester Airport and flew to New York City where she was to play the piano at Carnegie Hall. Carnegie Hall! Yes, Carnegie Hall! To play at Carnegie Hall was her life's goal and now she was given the chance, to hang her *Magnus opus* upon the great Wall of Life and be freed of dreaming, to be instead the dream. She looked dazzling, her dress was sapphire with glittering specks streaming down from her right shoulder and sweeping over in an ever-widening flow to the left. She had a cut up the left leg that was very high showing off her sexy legs and in her hair was a wreath of pine with a pinecone as the jewel in the crown. A blue ribbon weaved it into her deep brown hair. She addressed the crowd with a bow and she came up with diamonds in her eyes, and a *sleek radiance* that spewed from her very core. She was divine, she was all that heaven should be, and she spoke in motions of truths no book, no words, and no summation of God could compete with. She truly was out of this world, and the audience being alien, was awed by her very *prescience*. Her playing had moved them before she even touched a single key. She is so in tuned with her instrument that indeed, she became it. Her glory was an extension of the pianos, and each note possessed *itself*, with that *harmony*, she exuded naturally.

I stood in the back, dressed in my tuxedo we had picked up in the City when we arrived. Everything was so last minute, so rushed that night. I felt as if it was a dream and none of it happened. That was until I realized she was dead. I smoked a cigar (much to the displeasure of the ushers who kept coming over to me to tell me to put it out) I responded, *"I am an artist; it is natural that I disobey those subservient to me!"* Of course, I was punning on pretentiousness, but I do not think they got the joke. At least they did not think it was funny. I was drunk by the beauty of her playing and the presence of being involved in her life's dream felt a tingle throughout my body. This was what life was all about. I was there to share with her that morsel of existence when truth had its rule, when God swung down from the heavens and became seen. I saw God there that night. A most handsome creature, a powerful electric force he is, and he spoke to me. The words came out as music, and it was that of my beloved wife.

As she played her jazzed up Beethoven and reached the apex of the piece, I took out of my pocket her magnifying glass (she gave me before the performance as a present). I held it up and looked at her face with it. Tears streamed down my face, my stomach cramped up and I could feel her heat. I could taste her sugar; I could feel her entering my body with her *harmony*. The intensity struck me so vividly I almost dropped the glass, instead I put it in my pocket and, awestruck, studied her each histrionic roll of the head; my neglected cigar burning until it burned my hand and I dropped it on the floor.

A server came up the aisle and I grabbed some of the most delicious wine I had ever experienced. Perhaps it had nothing to do with the wine; maybe it was the *omnipotence* of the moment, the extreme grandeur of the evening. Either way, that wine gave me revolution! I sipped it readily, nurturing its *specific tang* with reluctant swallowing.

She finished her first piece; the crowd leapt up and roared with *marvel* at the *miracle* of her playing. I put the glass down and bellowed *that is my star! That is my star ever so bright, ever so illumine!* I clapped so heartily that I moved forward and almost tripped on the emotional string that entangled me. I felt pride leaking from every pore, from every clasp of hand, and from each hoorah; I screamed. A small child walked up to me, and pulled on my pant leg until I looked down at her. As soon as our eyes met time slowed to a frame-by-frame adrenalized motion and she said to me, *In pleno lumine. In posse!*[ii] *In posse! Eundo, morando, et reduendo!*[iii] *(In the full light of day. In potential! In potential! Going, remaining, and returning)*. This little angel was telling me that my wife was bound for a trip, all expenses paid. I, unaware of such foreknowledge, just smiled at the little kid as I tapped her out of the way. I lit another cigar, took another glass of wine and savored her next piece. I concentrated on her fingers as they *braved* her *courageousness*. Each comment her heart had to share with the world *resonated* through her playing. She enlightened the audience without their knowing, she perused their brains and, through music, installed the seed of hope. Before the song was over, that seed would flourish (if watered) into a flower. I knew this, for in my head grew a garden planted by the sun that is her *quintessence*. Anything with life could not help but be drawn to her *cloudlessness*. I evolved into a god; I grew so huge in the shadow of her spiritual penumbra, I felt my feet lift from the ground and I could swear I felt the flap of wings tapping upon my back. I felt a butterfly tear from the womb that grew inside me and flew away. Her elegance, her manipulation of how sound spilled into the ear was so incredible, I was convinced that glass should shatter. It did not, but it *felt* like it should. Perhaps that was the glass veneer I had hid behind all these years, mistaking words and ideas for the real thing, shattering. Exemplified in her *love,* her *admiration*, for being, feeling, experiencing, and making music not just heard and felt but making it a godly presence among men, she gave the audience more than they collectively could ever given her. Her gift was passion. She exemplified '*living the dream.*' She was the *dream*. She was *living*. I was dead and I was stretched and transcendent. *I* no longer defined *me*. It was *we, us, our*, it was *the universe.*

A man in a dapper suit bumped into me and I spilled my glass onto the floor. He kindly bent down to clean up the mess and asked if *I was ok. "I am very sorry indeed sir. Please forgive me. I was so caught up in her playing I in mid-step drifted off into some...well it sounds silly."* He gathered himself and the glass, and he stood up. *"Did you get any on you?"* I shook my head no and thanked him for his concern. He started to walk away when I started to say *that is my wife you know,* but my lips caught on themselves. He wandered off into the crowd and just before he was lost in the shuffle he turned back, looked at me, and mouthed, *lupus in fibula* (this is a person who disappears as they were being spoken off)...and I was pushed to the ground by some invisible force. Everything turned blurry and I blackout. When I came to there was a chubby man well dressed wearing a black blue-ribboned fedora and he smoked nervously from a maduro. *"Are you alright chap? Are you with us Sir? Hello there? He is coming too...Sir? Come on now you must come too."* I slowly opened my heavy eyelids and made out the form of the man and said, *"I didn't miss it did I? She is still playing yes?"*

*"No, no, no by all means you did not miss it?"* The round man chuckled. His eyes glistening and his cheeks blushing a bright crimson; *"that fine pianist is just taking a fifteen minute pardon, for it is intermission. Are you going to be all right then? I must get back to my seat if you are. You know, I can't leave the wife and kids alone too long!"*

I sat up and immediately started to look for the gentleman who had bumped into me, but he was nowhere to be found. I resolved that it was a phantasm that came as I was down. I was weary; I felt an inner *murkiness*, an impending *obscurity* lurking over me. My eyes stung, and my head boomed with insecurity. My hands turned clammy and I shivered uncontrollably. I was sure something was about to happen. Some terrible misfortune was creeping from behind. I just didn't know from which corner, from which *aspect* of my being. Was it outside of me? Was it about me or someone else? Or was I just being, well, silly?

I reached into my pocket and pulled out the magnifying glass, rolled it in my fingers and watched the ceiling twist and twirl in it. I was trying to distract my fears. I started to think of our most recent climb up the mountain, when she turned to me with the sunset behind her and she said, *give me your words, define me with your lips! Show me what the meaning behind passion is, without having to speak it. Let it slip off your lips with this kiss.* It was the most *radical* intimacy ever experienced between to lovers. She stopped, looked into my eyes with an appetency, a sleek eroticism that enkindled an ardor, a zeal for her to be inside my flesh. I wanted her to dive into me, so our souls could make fiery love. At this precise moment a meteor flashed across the sky, she collapsed into my arms, and we melted together in the warmth of the moonlight. We spoke nothing for the rest of the day. We just traded gazes of passionate *enthusiasm*. Like a river, we just flowed into a serene pool of bliss. Cooling, our heat kindly faded to embers and with the darkness we dissolved.

Her playing started again, it felt rushed, extreme, raging with *treachery*. I never before heard such tumult leak from her. She seemed distant; the keys seemed pained at her disregard. My heart raced, my blood was *furious*, choleric, indignant, and mad. My hands fumbled with the glass and again I was forced to put it in my pocket. I started to itch all over; I looked like a dog brushing at *his* infestation. My flesh slowly morphed into a thousand invisible spiders. My mouthed dried and my eyes became vague engines of *gloom*.

I could feel ghostly shadows spilling from the piano and down among the crowd. Their souls being slowly thawed as sand is from waves that eat at a lonesome island, wave-by-wave they allow themselves to be drawn in by her *extinction*. I could feel them, sweeping the floor away from me slowly. Death was here, his sickle, his decay, his eradication, extermination, extinguishment, extirpation, and his *liquidation*. The paradise had been lost to the sea, the heavens had risen up and we, the New Atlantis, had sunken beneath.

She pounded out the last few demons from her agent-to-the-vile and stood up with an irate wildness in possession of her body. Her hair veiling the insanity of her eyes, waving her hands impatiently about; her heavy breathing a symptom of her *crazed, enthusiastic, maniacal*, passion.

The audience threw themselves out of their seats and applauded her like they would a god, an emperor, a sultan, like she was their sacrificial savoir. She had given herself up for the good of the masses (or so it seemed to the audience). I knew better, but I also didn't know any different. I was lost in my own feelings for her, my own maniacal worship of her. She was already my savoir, why need I be a convert to these peoples religion? I mean, I know the Truth, I am righteous in Her, I am her other half, I am the embodiment and virtual her. I am her Christ, and I her Buddha. Come to me and I will tell you how *good* and *holy* she is. I am the illuminati, and I am illuminated in her.

I found myself running down the aisle in a frantic rush to pull my god from the false-praise of all these <u>idolaterers</u> (pun on adulterers) and for her sake prove to her I was her true, her one and only, her absolute apostle. I shall not deny her; I shall never turn my back onto her. That is when I tripped on my own legs just before reaching the stage. By the time I gathered myself and stood up, she had been taken off the stage. Only stagehands that were clearing all the roses and litter of their affections from the floor remained. I started to cry. I cried loud but no one cared. I wanted them to care, but they were too transfixed on my *wife* that they could not see that she was mine! She was all mine!

An hour passed, by which time I had relaxed and fixed myself with the tentative scraps of self-pity. I resolved to be supportive, to be selfless, to give praise unto her, and sacrifice whatever motives I welled up inside to save her glorious moment. She came out, a lantern of light that fearlessly begged the darkness to impede its virtuosity. She was so heavenly, I found myself upon my knees, saying *Oh goddess look upon me, I am your most adoring fan.* Or, *My love! How easy you make genius of mans simple modes of expression. You deify all ears that hear your art.*

She ran to me and said that we must go sit in a café somewhere, have some coffee and talk! She wanted to spend the evening walking the city, chatting like two Aristotle's about the magnificence of everything simple and *speck-tackular*.

## CAFÉ AFTER CONCERT
## PART TWO

I remember the air was so chummy, close, familiar, friendly, intimate, and real, that I sat back in my chair so comfortably I forgot I was human. I forgot that time and space dictated our lives, that a moment such as this one was passing, feral, a flicker. I lit a cigar, partook of it with such affection I almost caught fire from the cherry. I expelled my smoke and felt lifted as she looked at me from across the table.

I should have seen it then, I should have noticed that her brown eyes were so blue, that cracks had surfaced upon her eyes, but I decided to see tears, and I let her convince me they were of *"cheerfulness, felicity, gladness, happiness, joyfulness."* Pick one, she said with her words, but not with her eyes. I was so entrapped by her *message* that I became a prisoner to *innuendo* and *metaphor*. I could not see past the exterior of her phrases and the boldness of her adjectives, her eloquence, and her simplistic-complexity. I was so objective I objectified. I was so open, I left each door ajar, not realizing it isn't how many are open, but which ones. I turned her words, her message, into tools to define my own *desire* to *know* her. I wanted, and that is the seed that was my, her, our, destruction. She spoke *to be*, and I spoke, *to see*.

*I ain't gonna be a low down dog no more...* Meade "Lux" Lewis' *Low Down Dog* started to play over the cafe radio. She grabbed my hands and we got up and danced like 'old town boogie' high school sweethearts. An old couple in the far back clapped as we weaved in and out like intoxicated teenagers who snuck a bottle from the liquor cabinet. She had done it again. She eluded me. She shook me from my senses so I would stop reading the pages in her eyes that said, *Broken! Broken! I am Broken!*

Excitedly she dragged me by the hand into the busy streets. We, citystruck, gazed up at the dejected, depressed, desolate, dispirited, down; wait no, not down but downcast, downhearted, dull, dysphonic, heavy-hearted, buildings that stood erect like the phallic Truths humanity had learned to worship. They were like those annoying pop-ups that inquire if you wish to be *amplified*, broad, and more man than any woman could handle. No, we were clearly not city people, not like big city people. We loved New Hampshire. There brutality made the man manlier, the woman womanlier, and nature is not a park, it is not an artificial spectacle.

We looked down, eyes catching, and we smiled before falling into a joint laughter. We danced and skipped down the dreary lanes in the shadow of man's pride like a trickling echo. She traded her gold for my copper thoughts, and we fell in love again.

The flight back into Manchester was uneventful, she sleeping comfortably on my arm, her hands holding mine. She awoke as we touched down and her glowing eyes sunk my heart, I swallowed my fears, brushed her hair back, and kissed her on the forehead. We collected our baggage and, holding hands, got into a taxi to be taken home. We were so close to safety, so close to the creak of old mill doors and the rugged red luster of the brick mill walls that sang, *home!* So close, indeed, right now I can touch the littered halls with my feet and feel the sublime texture of familiarity, and in a speck, it all ended! There was no more home but only hospital. From the twisted metal and the clang of siren and emergency tools, came the bodies. The driver had been crushed beneath the bumper of an SUV and my wife was ejected and tossed onto the road. Dead, she was lifeless, breathless, and spiritless; she was gross, ugly, bloody, and vitality had become barren, and she gave no resemblance to she whom I had married.

Coming out of the romanticism, I opened my eyes and saw a tall gray stone before which I lay in a pile of fresh tossed dirt. My right hand outstretched, hurting from clenching a single red rose. I started to rise only to fall weakly to the ground. Catching a puff of dirt with my mouth, I gasp and spat it out. Meanwhile I extend an eye to study the stone. Upon it is her name. She was dead. With a moment of excited reverie, I rushed my hand into my pockets and in it was the magnifying glass. I pulled it up to my free eye and looked upon the grains of the stone. Crawling upon the tide of the rock was a ladybug. Sweetly she fluttered her wings and she brought a smile to my face. How small indeed, I thought, and yet how so very eternal, and how so very rare indeed is this thing we call life? This manifestation of moments that when frozen speak of infinite hope, infinite now!

I got up, smiling; I dusted myself off and walked off into the horizon, remembering what was, knowing it will always be, living within me.

FINIS

# The Switch Race

by Coleen
McCullough

Being poor, by which I mean having little more than what's monetarily necessary to stay afloat, can put a damper on planning and executing many family activities. I'm here to tell you however, that there are resourceful ways around most poor folk predicaments. I come from a family comprised of mostly farmers. As you can imagine, farmers tend to live in remote rural areas suitable for their agricultural endeavors but not much else. My family has mastered the art of family activities on a budget. After all, money or no, there aren't too many things you can pay to experience in such remote locations. I'm guessing that was the inspiration behind the scariest, I mean greatest game ever invented by one Martin McCullough, my grandfather.

It's called the switch race. Like the name suggests it's a race, a foot race to be exact. The competitors were Martin's grandchildren, myself included. The objective was to circle Grandpa's house at a speed not seen in average children in those days. No, we weren't a superior breed of family, we were driven by the incentive to outrun the wild-eyed former athlete, currently crazy old coot, wielding the willow switch, known as Grandpa. Usually the game would ensue after dinner during a large family get-together. The adults were relaxing after a hearty meal and the children were wound up after refueling on soda and dessert. Grandpa would turn his hearing aid down and attempt a nap in his Lazy Boy whilst the children would jump off the sofa spilling drinks and breaking valuables, clearly begging for a switch whipping, I mean race.

Grandpa, being the Patriarch of the family would see the need to move our rowdy behavior outside and took it upon himself to initiate a switch race. All children were strongly encouraged to participate by their fed up parents. They'd say, "Grandpa's put on a few pounds since the last time and I heard him say his knee was flarin' up earlier. That should shave a few seconds off his time." A handicap like that was enough to incite the kind of confidence it took to enter this type of contest. So as if our memory of sore muscles, stinging flesh, and blind hatred for Grandpa had banished completely, there we were, carefully choosing our switches. I followed suit of my cousins choosing a shorter switch to limit Grandpa's reach. Grandpa would laugh as if to imply, "You've selected the perfect switch! I've been training with a switch this exact measurement for months!" Then we'd nervously hand our switch to Grandpa and line up for the race.

Cousins, siblings, and unsuspecting invited guests took there mark. "Ready Set," Jimmy was already crying and Tate had prematurely started on a wild run spooked by Jimmy's sobs. "Go!" The adults, as convincing as they had been earlier, were clearly not on our side. Aunt Sharma's tip to Grandpa "The freckly one's getting away! Git'em!" left us with no doubt that we had been tricked into a whippin' disguised as a fun family custom. The race was on. Grandpa, like most villainous characters portrayed in horror flicks, kept a slow non threatening, yet steady pace while grandchildren tripped all over themselves trying to make their legs run faster. One by one though Grandpa would lick the backs of our calves, thighs and rumps with that damned switch (I knew that switch was too long)! He'd say "HA! Gotcha!" Sometimes preemptively he'd say it and the grandchild would just stiffen up and fall over as if he'd already been struck. This was greatly amusing to our parents. They were so consumed by laughter they were seizing to breath.

Once you were struck, your run was over unless you were fool enough to jump back in. My cousin Eric was just that kind of a fool. He was the fastest of the bunch and could no doubt run circles around Grandpa. His lanky build was perfect for long evasive strides. Grandpa would always appear defeated complete with indignant-expression as Eric would pick up the pace just before Grandpa could strike. The disqualified grandchildren sat next to their snickering parents cheering for their hero, Eric. Eric would get cocky too. He'd slow it down, speed it up, and hi-five the losers on the sidelines. That would only provoke Grandpa to cheat. Grandpa would let Eric turn a corner and curse at him for effect. Then he'd wait there, right where Eric had left him until Eric would come back around and have to face Grandpa head on. Needless to say, Grandpa always won and Eric was the only Grandchild with switch marks on his shins. Oh, good times! Now, back to my point. All we needed to engage in some family fun was each other, a willow switch, some antibiotic ointment to speed healing, and the commitment of a maniacal old man to keep his family close (and subdued) on hardly any money (Ointment 3.99 at most drug stores).

# POLITICS

# Theory Now!

### By: Mark T. Fitzpatrick

### <u>Clash Of Nothing, End Of Nothing: Fixations of Civilizations</u>

Measuring out how "democratic" a society is or mapping out the "clashing civilizations" is equivalent to the measuring of human skulls: it is political eugenics. Of course, eugenics was a political creation: the biases of Europeans manufacturing the "inferiory" of Africans and Asians. But this power relation exists today. We live in a time where many analysts will cry at the mutating of Europe into "Eurabia" and the meeting at the "bloody" borders between the Judeo-Christian world (yeah, those two *naturally* come together) and Islam. Political scientists have always jumped the gun at analyzing certain situations, whether it was the Cold War or welfare policy. However, this has gone to a new level.

These new political eugenicists include people like James Pinkerton of *Newsday*. Pinkerton wrote recently in the *American Conservative* on the "heroic" need for the "Knights of the West" to stand against Islam. Using the almost Hellenic orientalism of Tolkien's *Lord of the Rings*, he writes that the "self-defense in one's own area—the homeland, which he calls the Shire" is a strategy the West should adopt. Why should it adopt it? Because the "Muslimization [of] Europe, [would have] consequences [that] would be catastrophic for Americans". Pinkerton lays out arguments that the increasing Muslim populations of Europe, many of which could be from fundamentalist branches, would destroy the land of "Aesop and Aristotle" as the Taliban did to Buddhism in Afghanistan.

Pinkerton is definitely trained in the primordialist school of political science. Pinkerton argues how Tolkien appreciated the fact that certain "creatures" inhabit naturally their own lands (Hobbits should live in the Shire for example). The geographic essentialism is painfully apparent. Who in their right mind thinks all human beings from this planet naturally come from their own location and should do "their own thing" (Pinkerton's words)? This idea totally ignores human migration, trans-nationalism, the banality of nation-states and even the fact we are all equal human beings as human beings. I am not arguing for some sort of humanism, but to say, for example, the Chinese should stay in China because China is for the Chinese is ludicrous. Equally idiotic is Pinkerton's hypocrisy toward our own nation-state: by Pinkerton's logic, the English should never have colonized the US, which has now become the last light of the West according to Pinkerton and others like him. Following from that, colonization should never have happened, one of the main tools of how many parts of the world are still in the periphery Third World, seems like his argument might be good for something!

So human beings should have their place(s) in the world and we should brutally guard our borders in a Greco-epic like fashion? I guess so; Pinkerton even praises the recent film *300*, which was brutally laced with racism, orientalism, and even historical lies. The Spartans, unfortunately for some moviegoers and graphic novelists, were not the beckons of "freedom". If you really want their philosophy, you should be sending your 8-year-old boys to the military, begin enslaving "barbarians" and end suffrage for women. Back to Tolkien's since Pinkerton spends most of his article on him.

Again, Pinkerton writes about his so-called "Shire strategy". It is the humble defense of the homeland against the infringements of other civilizations that do not know their "place" in some sort of primordial geography. Pinkerton also takes out from Tolkien those Catholic-laced discourses Tolkien has as something to look toward. Tolkien admitted *Lord of the Rings* was a very Catholic book. Because of this, Pinkerton makes the claim that the Shire strategy should be an argument for Christendom. Pinkerton finds this universal path, Christendom, more enlightening that the Hegelian/End-of-History arguments of Francis Fukuyama or the neo-liberal rants of Thomas Friedman. In the post-9/11 world, the Shire/Christendom strategy is needed according to Pinkerton.

What I find most disturbing about this path is its excuses for war, fixed borders and fetishment toward culture and civilization. Pinkerton is critical of neo-conservatives for attacking Europe rhetorically, especially when it has come to Europe's criticisms of US foreign policy. Instead, Pinkerton wants the US to embark on a cultural crusade, protecting "Europa" and defining Europe more precisely. This means not including the Muslim-populated Turkey into the European Union but includes the expansion of the EU to the Ural Mountains, the so-called "natural" dividing line of the East/West. The US must do this humbly, not acting like Sauron or the Roman Empire in making some "New World Order" like Fukuyama has argued. Harking back to the violence of Europe, Pinkerton seems to want Europe to be militarized toward the "invading Muslim armies" (such as King Charles Martel of the Franks in the Battle of Tours).

If you have not noticed how ridiculous Pinkerton's arguments are becoming, he goes full speed ahead with some amazingly out-there ideas. For the low-birthrates of Europe, he suggests that the European-descendents of the American continent, such as in Argentina, Chile, Uruguay, Canada and Brazil, return to Europe, so that Muslim populations can dwindle. He also says Europe should geo-politically pick its battles. For example, he says the Ukraine and Russia should focus on the Muslim populations of the Tatar, Kazak and other Central Asian peoples. Pinkerton also argues the European Union needs to accept and incorporate its Christian and Christendom history so they can become united as a civilization. Way to make a transnational economic and military organization more than it should be! "The West shall stay the West" Pinkerton proclaims, even though the "West" never completely existed to the Greeks, Romans or the Germanic tribes but until the Great Schism disconnected Catholics from Orthodox Byzantium.

Pinkerton's theory involves the building of walls to separate Europe from Asia (no more Eurasia I guess). This would help stop "Eurabia" and keep "Europa" the virgin, female flower she is, ready to be protected by patriarchal, Greco-epic heroes who would penetrate her culturally rich and pure European vagina in the name of "freedom" later. This is basically what Pinkerton is saying. He is mythologizing the idea of a Europe, essentializing and primordializing geo-political positions of peoples to make their civilizations "stay in there place," and fetishizing the homeland as something that needs to be culturally pure for the citizens of arbitrary borders. He is also cutting up the world map, suggesting the American continent must go help Europe since we are the colonial abortion of Europe. Russia must include itself in Europe and not some Asian Union (which it is part of) to control its Muslim populations (Tatars, Chechens and other peoples the Tsars imposed themselves on over the last 500 years). Pinkerton then suggests a Tolkeinian "Council of Elrond" where this new Christendom goes into Africa to stop Muslims from attacking Christians. He remarks this would help establish a new Nicene Creed such as the Council of Nicaea did back in the 300s.

Not only is he seeped in herofication by taking bits of history and wrapping paradigms of Occident vs. Orient, Pinkerton wants to make a strategic "Clash of Civilizations". This term also came in the post-Cold War world along with the term "End-of-History". The "End-of-History", a term accredited to Fukuyama, argued that the beat of historical progress had ended with the conflict of the US and Soviet Union now gone. Instead, a new world without history (for you Hegelian-Marxists out there, you know conflict = progress = history) has begun with the US as a super-hegemon, never before seen on the planet. Hence, all economic and social constructs can be constructed by the US (ex. globalization as neo-liberal).

The term "Clash of Civilizations" came from the political scientist Samuel Huntington, who saw nothing but problems over the horizon for the US. Instead of Fukuyama's US-Empire optimism, Huntington thought that without a central conflict between a hegemon and a pretender-hegemon, the cultural politics of the world would be empowered and enhanced on the international stage. Thus, "civilizations" would war with other civilizations within basic international relations structures (balance of power, imperialism, hegemony). Within such a paradigm, however, Huntington shows his racism, colonialist sentiments, essentialism and orientalism. His ten civilizations are compartmentalized as follows: 1) The West, 2) The Orthodox, 3) Latin America, 4) Islam, 5) Hindu civilization, 6) Sinic civilization, 7) Japan, 8) Sub-Sahara Africa, 9) Buddhist civilization, and the 10) Lone countries: Israel, the Caribbean, etc. For Huntington, the post-Cold War vindicated his postulates, due to the genocides in former Yugoslavia between West-Orthodox-Muslim factions, conflicts in Russia (Orthodox-Islam), Pakistan-Indian conflicts (Hindu-Islam) and 9/11 (West-Islam). Balance of power seems to be the game in town for Huntington since international organizations such as the United Nations are purely "Western concepts". Thus, civilizations vie for power over world politics. In our times, Sinic and Islam civilizations are challenging the West's overall dominance.

Although he centrally agrees with Huntington, Pinkerton wants the "Clash of Civilizations" better formulated and not hijacked by neo-conservative angst. However, his desires are equally as distressing as the neo-cons: Pinkerton's paradigm is a world so compartmentalized and essentialized I am confused already! To argue that Islam and The West, as civilizations, naturally are enemies is dangerous since it ignores the history of interactions between religions and naturalizes the relationships of ideas. Ideas do not have natural relationships; to argue the "nature of things" (this is not a criticism of Lucretius) or better, the natural connections of ideas, is dangerous. Ideas do not happen, nor are they from linear connections; they result from particular *episteme* or paradigms that historically are particular and wrapped with several discourses, ideologies and hegemonic-thinking. Hence, no ideas (whether they are religions or civilizations) can be antagonistic toward each other since full out maps of those ideas are often never completely understood or formed. I am not saying things can never be argued, but to naturalize two ideas and then to say they are antagonistic is a very bad analysis. For example, many people have said that somehow Marx or Marxism were antithecal to neoclassical economics (such as Adam Smith or David Ricardo). Anyone who has read any intro to economic thought books realizes that such a statement is utterly silly and empty of actual historical analysis. One would find Marx would not exist without Smith and that they were very much in agreement with many economic principles.

Similar to the last points, it is impossible to make up a civilization. A civilization is far too an umbrella concept to be thought as one defining concept or ideas. The "West" is a rainbow of ideas that often have no connections to each other (Greco-Roman, Catholic-Protestant, Germanic-Romantic, etc). So is the Islamic world, which in many ways is far more Western than many Westerners would like to admit and far too various within itself. For example, how are Indonesians that related or connected to Saudis for example? If you say religion, then I, who was raised Catholic, am connected on a civilization level with all other Catholics throughout the world, whether it be Africa, Asia or Oceania? I am definitely connected to everyone just by being human, but my experiences as a human being are radically different from another person found in some other "civilization". And religion is never picture-perfect. In Catholicism itself, disputes between liberation ideology in Latin America often were met harshly by the Vatican while being embraced by local Catholic priests fighting off communist and contra forces in their home countries.

There is also an arbitrariness of what Huntington and Pinkerton would designate as a "civilization". For example, identity is a many multi-faceted thing. As Amartya Sen would point out, I can describe myself in so many ways: born from the middle class, white-Irish, Roman Catholic-raised, educated at private school, college-educated, male, brother, son, raised in Essex county Massachusetts, living in Hampshire county Massachusetts, owner of many wealth commodities such as a car and computer with internet, beer and coffee aficionado, etc. Sure, often identity politics can be critiqued by the Right or Left for its dividedness, but by revealing the arbitrariness of identity, it often seems that "culture" and "nation" are revealed as very malleable ideas then. Hence, to say a civilization is from a certain connection or geography ignores the particularness of any sort of culture. Sure, Huntington has this "lone country" category to talk about countries that have multifaceted connections, but any country has a multifaceted nature. The differences between the US and Canada or with Europe is huge; so why are we all stuck together. Why is not Mexico part of the West either? Mexico's influence on US culture is the same, if not greater, than Canada's. Yet, Mexico is part of "Latin America". Moreover, Argentina, Brazil, Chile are mostly Spanish-Italian-Portuguese, why are they part of Latin America? Japan and China are definitely different societies and cultures, but civilizations? Huntington includes Korea and Vietnam with the Sinic civilization, but many Japanese find connections between themselves and those two nation-states. Yes, identity, nation and culture are arbitrary but they are serious issues, especially since they are being politically aligned against their wills with other peoples, they might not have any connections with besides with being human. Here's Huntington, some white dude from Harvard, talking about how Africans go with this civilization, the Japanese go with this civilization, Muslims go here, etc. The arbitrariness and control is dangerous, compartmental and laced with racism, or at least, huge assumptions about other races and cultures.

Although Pinkerton and Huntington would say this process does not exist, arguably globalization does disprove their overall paradigm. The overall connectedness of the world, beyond economics is apparent these days. Hence, conflicts, which do happen, can happen for other reasons besides civilization differences. One belief is the arguments against modernity. Whether they are neo-Luddites or Al-Qaeda, the technological and social advances that are pushed in a global order, especially from the dominance of the West, is seen threatening for some; so one particular terrorist organization, for one of many reasons, attacks the US because the US is seen as the main pusher. Now that is one aspect and one argument, but it enlightens the overall perspective on our current social reality.

Besides the aspects of the anti-globalization forces that are mainly anti-neo-liberal or anti-Western, the main issue is that globalization proves the malleableness of culture. Because of increased inter-connectedness, how can one say that there are these "civilizations" existing in their own vacuums? To use Pinkerton, how then can societies and civilizations "stay where they are" since the only real nature of human beings that I am comfortable in saying is that we never stay in one place for very long! To argue that civilizations stay in their place ignores immigration and migration, both ancient and contemporary, and especially in the US's history. Pinkerton would probably be foaming at the mouth back in the 1800s when the Irish migrated over to the US, "destroying" American civilization. Sure, the Irish have been co-opted into the "American" paradigm, but not every ethnicity or culture needs to be normalized or "naturalized" into the United States. Nor do we need a multicultural society, since multiculturalism is often argued by elites wanting the fetishment of other cultures while disenfranchising the political will of the immigrant group. The ideal would be transnational cosmopolitanism, which is the ideal of globalization-without-labels, where a cultural or ethnic group can enter a country and have the political power of any other citizen without being zoologically placed in a citizen hierarchy against the "natural" citizens of that nation-state. This argument, along with the identity argument, shows how culture and civilization are malleable especially in a globalized world. To say there is even a "civilization" out there with some Other-Same paradigm becomes ludicrous.

However, did 9/11 end globalization? The answer is no. New ways to express the world are now occurring, that are beyond some Hegelian "progress" or neo-liberal, WTO order. As previously stated, 9/11 could be the effects of individuals and organizations lashing out at the ideologies dominating the forms of globalization that is occurring. Obviously, globalization does not need to be neo-liberal. Although many of the protesters in Seattle back in 1999 argued against globalization as an occurrence, many argued that globalization should not be co-opted by neo-liberal economics. Hence, globalization can occur both beyond economic viewpoints and beyond Western, neo-liberal structures of free trade, deregulation and dissolved trade barriers.

Finally, probably the strongest critique of Pinkerton can come from Huntington himself. Huntington has moderated his views slightly since publishing most of his works on the "Clash of Civilizations". He argues that essentially all religions are mostly peaceful and that if one were to measure the political violence of a religion over time, Christianity would be over Islam. However, the strongest methodological critique Huntington gives would be that populations clash with other populations only because of youth and poverty, or the youth bulge theory. The lower median population for age and the lower development index of a country often creates a generation of young people so disenfranchised, any ideology that seems to be liberating is attractive. Fascism served the youth of Germany and Italy quite well before and during World War II so too do fundamentalist branches of any religion serve the youth of poor countries as an emotional cushion during trying times.

So, what is left of Pinkerton? I can honestly see Pinkerton hanging out in his basement playing Dungeon and Dragons using characters to represent Christendom and others to be Muslims. His ideas ultimately fail: he compartmentalizes the world as clashing civilizations, with one needing to defend itself "heroically" against the other. His Shire strategy continues the orientalism found in the West since the Greeks by violently and preemptively imposing on itself paradigms of control and difference. Like the late, great Edward Said has pointed out, Pinkerton and others like him legitimate and naturalize everything from patriarchy to racism by manufacturing imagined communities and geographies across the world. Politics between peoples become heightened to levels of possible war and genocide by boxing in "civilizations" desiring the protection of pure, virgin homelands. The peoples of those homelands are often made up along the way, through myths, racist ideology, and instrumentalist control by any dominant paradigm or group. Pinkerton's Tolkienian international relations fantasies will lead all of us down a path as dark as the times of Middle Earth, but will not make heroes of anyone, any day.

**James Pinkerton's article can be found in the September 10th issue of the *American Conservative*. I also have a link where it can be viewed: http://www.amconmag.com/2007/2007_09_10/cover.html**

*Mark Fitzpatrick is a graduate of the University of Massachusetts at Amherst. There, he gained his BA in political science with a concentration in political theory. He has also studied aspects of philosophy and anthropology, gaining interests in the history of ideas and critical theory. Born in Lawrence, MA, he currently resides in Amherst, MA, preparing for his attendance at graduate school. He can be reached for further inquiries and questions at fitzmarc@hotmail.com.*

# PROSE/SATIRE/ESSAY

## *Reality TV: Electronic Heroin*

By Gary "The G-man" Toms

There are times when I seriously wonder if I need a psychiatric evaluation. I tend to think I have more issues than Playboy. I say this because I often fantasize about doing certain things to certain people I see on television. I get an enormous sense of pleasure from these thoughts, and I've come to realize that I'm indirectly lashing out against a blatant attempt at mind-control by various network "kingpins". Let me give you a few examples of what I mean. Perhaps you guys and gals have felt these urges as well.

No kingpin is more capable of altering your mental or physical state than President George W. Bush. Think about it. You're either scratching your head trying to figure out what the hell he just said, or you become so emotional over his policies and/or initiatives that you literally shake. Whenever I see him on the tube giving some moronic speech, I imagine running up to the podium and mushing him in the face with a pie made of rotted cheese and eggs. I don't mean some light-hearted mush either. I mean the type of mush that makes your neck and whole body jerk backward. Call it a mush with conviction. Then, doing my best Gilbert Gottfried impersonation, I'd yell, "There's your piece of the tax cut pie, 'Georgie Boy!'" I'm sorry, but the man just irritates me to no end. I'd rather watch reruns of that hideous Kathie Lee Gifford movie that premiered on the "E!" network years ago. It was so bad I can't even remember the title. Nor do I want to. Someone pass me a barf bag. Kelly Ripa, you rock!

"*The O'Reilly Factor*", on the Fox News Channel, is one of those shows that attempt to get you "hooked".... on stupidity. I would love to appear as a commentator just to irk the hell out of Bill O'Reilly. Can you get anymore smug than this guy? He never lets you get a word in edgewise. I've often imagined myself on the set playing with an "Etch-A-Sketch" and asking him if he liked my stick figure drawings as he mercilessly grilled his guest. If that didn't work, I'd keep asking him why Tim Russert of "*Meet the Press*" was so much smarter than he was. I don't know what's more annoying. Having to watch O'Reilly or taking a dump and realizing you've run out of toilet paper! If he likes confrontation, I'd give him confrontation. The big wuss!

How many damn cooking shows do we need? You've already got *Emeril*, Rachel Ray, some British chick with pretty nice tits, *The Naked Chef, The Iron Chef, The Manic-Depressive Chef* (it's not the chopped onions that's making the poor bastard cry) and a host of others that continue to provide a "fix". I miss the days when there were just two cooking gods, Julia Child and Graham Kerr. Kerr was the man! The best part of watching "*The Galloping Gourmet*" was waiting to see if Kerr would be sauced long before the meat was at the end of the show. It seemed like the man took a sip of wine every three minutes while cooking.

As far as my fantasy goes in these cases, I'd call myself "*The Disgruntled Chef*." Instead of preparing lavish meals or exquisite desserts, I'd pull out a box of Cheerios, a can of Ravioli, or a Popsicle and slam it on the counter. I'd look right into the camera and say, "I don't cook, damn it! Neither should you!" I'd knock over all the ingredients and spices, kick chairs, curse like a sailor on weekend leave, hurl utensils at the crew, and squirt cheese dip all over the audience. I may not get much in the way of a studio audience, but I'll bet the ratings would go through the roof.

The fashion-related programs are a major pain in the ass too. Celebrities like Joan Rivers, whose repeated plastic surgery has earned her the name "*Catwoman*", create legions of junkies by telling you to wear this or that because it's "in". Versace, Valentino, Donna Karan, Gucci, Phat Farm, Roca-Wear, Fetish and Sean John are some of the brands shoved in our faces week after week. What's worse is the fact that we are made to feel less than adequate if we don't buy their stupid products. Shut up and go away with your overpriced crap! You know what my favorite label is? It's called <u>affordable</u>!

I'd love to show up on these programs in ripped up jeans with mustard stains on them and my butt cheeks hanging out where the back pockets should be. I'd walk on set looking like a bad version of the artist known as Prince. I'd wear a white tee-shirt with dried-up yellow stains in the underarm area and some really horrendous smelling sandals. I'd make sure I didn't bathe for a week before going on the show too. I'd give whole new meaning to the term "funky fashion". Then, I'd smack Joan Rivers and her snotty fashion panelists upside the head with one of my dirty sandals and run like I stole something.

With all that said, you can now draw you own conclusion. Maybe I'm a little psycho, or maybe I'm just crazy like a fox. Whatever the case, I'm sure that I'm not alone when it comes to having such thoughts. If you do as well, count yourself as one of the lucky ones. With so many networks offering you a free "hit", you've made the decision not to let anyone tap your intelligence vein or alter your state of consciousness. Our desperate need for instant gratification, acceptance and escapism helped create these media drug lords. They've become a major part of our culture. We're so addicted to them that our brains are literally rotting, and the brain matter is beginning to ooze from our ears. People all over the world cannot seem to live without reality television, and the remote control is the needle that injects this poison into our veins.

# The Irish Eyes of Jimmy O'Reilly

By Gary "The G-man" Toms

It seems like it was yesterday when I graduated from Far Rockaway High School. The class of '81 was a very special class. It was the year the school took the title of "High School of the Year," and we received the award because of high academic achievements by the majority of our graduating class and the exceptional career-oriented programs that had been developed. The New York State Health Assistant Program was one of them. Ms. Barbara Jackson, R.N., an extraordinary human being, was the director of the program, and the course offered training in the nursing and medical assistant fields. If I'm not mistaken, the course is still in progress to date. However, Ms. Jackson retired from the program some time ago. This program offered me a glimpse of what the medical profession was all about.

I started at the beginning of the school year in 1977, shortly before I developed *"The Fever"* for Saturday nights. As part of the program, we were trained to perform certain medical procedures, such as taking blood pressure, height and weight measurement and testing blood sugar levels. During the course of the school week, we would be assigned to the Queens Nassau and Surfside Nursing Homes, in Far Rockaway, NY, to assist in the care of patients. It was one of the most rewarding periods of my life. It ranked right up there with my role as Borough Commander for the Queens Chapter of the New York City Guardian Angels, a volunteer organization that helps patrol the subway system. What made my experience at Surfside Nursing Home even more memorable was my relationship with an elderly Irishman by the name of Jimmy O'Reilly.

The program stipulated that we had to maintain a journal on the patients we cared for and how we assisted them during our visits. When I was assigned to "Jim-Jim," as I lovingly referred to him, I did not know what to expect. I was taught that certain patients have certain temperaments, and we had to deal with them in a professional manner, even if they went as far as to spit on us. The image of someone hurling a phlegm ball at me was very discouraging, but I forged ahead. To this day, I consider that decision a blessing.

Jim-Jim was 85 years old, balding, extremely frail and blind. The first time I walked into his room, I saw him sitting in what the nurses had described as his favorite chair. He was leaning toward his right side, as he always did, due to his frail condition. His mouth was open just enough to view a small portion of his tongue, and he trembled slightly. At that moment, something happened to me that changed my life. I felt an intense need to care for this man. It was the same feeling that made me join the Guardian Angels.

In the weeks that passed, I looked forward to spending time with him, and I anxiously jotted down the particulars of what we did that day in my journal. I remember vividly how I would try to teach him the words to *"Rapper's Delight"* by the Sugar Hill Gang, and he would counter by singing an old Irish hymn. I relished these sessions because the nursing staff, and Ms. Jackson, stated, "He doesn't talk to anyone! Jimmy's always quiet!" Despite this fact, we shared some very funny moments. Conversations were difficult at times because he was often disoriented, and he would forget what he was going to say most of the time. I know this bothered him a lot, and I could see the frustration and sadness in his eyes whenever it happened. I always made it a point to smile and touch his hand whenever it did.

There were many times when he would mention the wonders of Ireland, but he never mentioned what part he was from. That's still a mystery to me. I know he loved growing up there and missed it a great deal. Although our communicating was difficult, I got close enough to notice that when it rained, he would sit by the window to listen. A tear would always fall from his left eye. I wanted to ask him why he cried whenever the heavens opened up, but something told me not to. I don't know why, but I always felt it had something to do with a long lost love. This too is a mystery to me.

The school months were passing quickly, and sessions with Jim-Jim were becoming a crucial part of my life. It was getting to the point that I would go by the nursing home outside of school hours just to check on him. The nurses were always accommodating, and I was happy if I just got to see him for a quick minute.

It was nearing the end of the school year, and we would have to submit our journals to Ms. Jackson for review. I was excited about the relationship I had built with this man, and I suspected that Ms. Jackson would be overjoyed as well. After all, that's what the Health Assisting program was all about. It was the middle of the week, and I arrived at Surfside for my weekly visit. I entered Jim-Jim's room and noticed that his bed was empty and sheetless. I assumed that maybe he took ill and had to be rushed to the hospital. I inquired about his whereabouts, but the nurses were vague in their answers. I turned to head back to Jim-Jim's room, and I saw Ms. Jackson approaching me. I started to tremble, and I could not stop. I asked her where Jimmy was, and in a calm, warm, almost motherly tone she said, "He died last night Gary." At that point, I walked back into his room. I took a deep breath to see if I could still smell a trace of the ointment the nurses would place on his wounds. I knelt down by his favorite chair, and I started to cry until my stomach hurt. At times, I still cry.

Nearly 25 years later, now that I have a far better understanding of human relationships, I realize that Jimmy O'Reilly had an enormous impact on my life. I often asked myself, "If he had not been blind, would we have been as close?" If he could've seen my black skin, would he have shared as much about his culture and homeland? You see, when you grow up watching the Ku Klux Klan march through your town, or witness black people being brutalized in history books and during the civil rights period, you can't help but question the mindset or actions of those who are white or have white skin tone.

Recently, as I stood in front of the Surfside Nursing Home reminiscing about him, I was finally able to answer those questions. It would not have mattered at all because we needed each other. He needed me in order to connect to someone as his final days approached, which I suspect he knew were upon him, and I needed him to help mould me to become a sensitive, loving and compassionate man. I was sixteen at the time and Jim-Jim undoubtedly had a significant role in my development as a young man. My relationship with Jim-Jim showed me that the only boundaries that exist between people are those that are deliberately placed because of fear, stupidity and sheer ignorance. We all will die someday, and if you are fortunate enough to have a total stranger with you at that moment, the race of the person certainly will not matter. No one wants to die alone, and although many of us attempt to dismiss the point, we all need each other in some way, shape or form. Thank you for teaching me that Jim-Jim. I love you, I miss you, and I pray that you will rest in peace…. forever.

## **Pale Memory.**

    Blue haze slowly metamorphoses hills into rosy giants above gray sands. Light becomes alive, enlarges into a faint aura, disarming the ominous mountain range across the valley.

    The animal within awakens to the pale glow; the eye, afraid to miss the wonder that engulfs, searches toward the East, as if life itself emanated from that point in primal dawn; still so near, yet impalpable, swelling into reality in the breast of the beholder.

    The great phalanges of a headless sphinx evolve out of the morn, foreboding on the bare flanks of a hillside. Shapes move faster than mind, colors define and redefine a continuous dance of vanishing nocturnal demons.

    Joshuas, arms reaching up above man and ass, darkly praising aurora-multiforma, the sky now a perfect cupola of opaque grays. The path, a winding animal, creeping narrowly to infinite hardness in the arid peaks afar.

    I watch from the shadow of what was night impenetrable a fraction of time ago, and seek the spirit of those who once, like myself, hunted in these desertic hills. I find awe in pantheistic respect for continuum, here on this ground, between the Ute and the deer consciousness; perpetually in perennial precarity I, proud ignorant, am but a frying pan away from silent nets at tribal hunts. We, are but a gun away from those who survived; our knowledge, once removed from understanding.

    I, breathe reverence at dawn, I smell fear at breakfast; ever concerned, ever aware: the masculine spirit of the hunter pervades volcanic rock, femina dries up among cacti, to feed but the toughest of animals, in the hardest of climes.

    Here I begin anew, with yet another dawn over the pale gray sage.

    With absurdian contemplation, I expound on man's demise. Raccoon paws clicking away in logorrheic syncopation. I play with your language till spontaneously expurgating daily horror by the ream. Common sense trumps intellect in incongruity.

Survival, my specialty, I find excitement in a sclerotic world. Sanity? Never - solace? Perhaps. My only promise is to intuit and follow the needs I perceive in the reader's comments. Sharing artful stimulus is the ultimate goal here.

A feminine analyst, sitting atop the garden fence, I muse at the machinations of man. Perennially awed by the power of the environment to overcome most assaults upon it's temper. All I offer is a vast empiric experience. Emerging from a European Cro-Magnon consciousness and having survived years in the American deserts, I can only guarantee an unsettling experience.

    People cling to me for security and a bit of insurance. My role is to assuage their fear of doom and famine (they all know that I can find a dandelion in hell) and they would never starve in my company.

May I feed, fulfill, amuse or arouse till the winds dry my carcass.

*** Nadine Sellers is a French writer and spoken word artist. She resides in the belly of the whale, the prairie states of America; and pours senses onto the pages of her future.

# Up To The Aumbries With You

By Daniel Scott Batten

The rain comes and my soul is wash with restraint – wash with ease and somehow within this comfort lives a vicious sense of tumult. My mind yearns not for solitude; it yearns for excess. A kind of excess that unfolds its golden wings and overshadows me, and looming overhead, it exhausts me. It made the air thick with its disdain. After consuming me with its luster, I seek to touch and there I catch my bane. A feeling starts to morph into a rash. A rash that is insistent on being itched. So, I, like the human machine, I follow my orders. I itched until the rash bled, and caught by the pain, I gazed out my window for sympathy.

A cool breeze summoned me, its voice was harsh and scratchy, and confused I started to cry out for mercy, but the audience of my room told me not to speak – they put their frigid hands over my lips and hushed me with a lullaby into a hypnotic sleep. "Dream," they'd say, "Dream until living is a dream. Dream until everything seen and heard is dead. Dead like life! Dead like the feelings that consume us with the fire of our thoughts; thoughts that like wood are burned into ash. Dream, dream and become a corpse and let the dirt of reality pile onto your grave. Rise like a ghost and go to the light and be free!"

Groggy, I felt something trying to break loose within me, something suppressed was raging into fire, a fire that made my flesh want to fall away from my bones.

## Panes subcinericeos
## (Bread Baked In The Ashes)

By Daniel Scott Batten

It always seems the most achieved in society speak with *learning* about the topic of suffering. They turn the word *suffering* into concepts and divide it up into categories and degrees. It becomes a means of weights and measures. It becomes scientific, just another specimen that is studied in pieces and thoughts are formed around these theories of why each subcategory deviates from the other. The greatest scholars of psychology spend a decade in school to understand the minutest strands of the human condition; physiologists and physicians spend years and years studying the functions of a single organ. Biochemists and neurologists spend entire lives dedicated to understanding DNA and pontificating on the structure of *structure*. Physicists write volumes and volumes where they eloquently banter between themselves about the properties of elements and talk about the atom, and yet, not ONE has ever even seen an atom. Just as protons disappear when observed, so does any understanding of something when it is categorized to please the bias of one understanding. It is most satisfying for the aristocrat to measure and weigh the suffering of others, and speaking in its honor, and it is another for them to know anything about it. They can study it, they can talk to a million people *they* deem to be victims of *suffering*, and yet, ultimately all they are proving is that they suffer from a lack of suffering. It is not words, it is not bound by gravity, and it is not as easily isolated as an organ, or a DNA strand. Suffering is not something to be understood, nor is it something to categorize and to accuse with. Suffering in all its forms is valid and there are no member carrying cardholders, for it is not exclusive, or maybe it is and that is why we suffer still.

# I AM CANTABRIGIERSIS: IF YOU MUST KNOW

### By Daniel Scott Batten

I tip my hat too you, oh laborious hephaestian helots;[iv] and to the genitive synergies[v] and *contra mundum*[vi] snubbers, who are so happy to wear emblems and crosses whereas I am contented with the badge, *et ipse/Notus in frates animi paterni(And for myself known for my fatherly concern for my brothers.).*[vii] I am well informed by armchair discoursers and Philistine-philosophers of those prescriptions conceived to impregnate the world with the University. I have betrayed many notions to this clever claptrap of convention, joining in with the silliness of the Oxfords, beating the bounds and tray-tripping my Latinized origin, *Cantabrigiersis!*[viii] It is a great heavenly joke to make men strive by education to be of a higher nature, to be better suited for praise and earthly things to be blown up in a sentence; *Nihil sanantibus litteris* ('Such erudition has no power to heal').[ix] It may seem the stray ordinance of soul to have a need to seek out a fellow Cambridge man,[x] when in the end we are all just cigarless youths[xi] pondering the spaces between atoms and all the while finding ourselves ignorant to *God*. It seems the occupation of many mild-minds to smoke God and in their euphoria find need to preach their insignificant moralities; all the while, they talk themselves out of living, for salvation. I am clearer than this in my faith and my education is mine, I shall love those that sit by this fire of mind, but I shall not bend myself to their metals. I am a Cambridge man, if you must boast of Universities, then find a boulder off some trail in the mountains and tell it how huge and macroscopic you are! See if it shudders in your presence, silly, silly man, so trite that you can't see past your own nose, the world that is so vast and small in comparison still!

# *PLAYS*

## *Half-Way There:*
## *Bitch Adenaka's Buddha*

### A One Act Stageplay
by
p.l. frank

## Half-Way There:
*Bitch Adenaka's Buddha*

Cast of Characters

**ACT I**

Izzo (Halfway House resident)

Spencer (Halfway House resident)

Coffee shop patron #1

Coffee shop patron #2

Coffee shop patron #3 *(optional; can also be a dual-role w/ Mrs. Adenaka)*

Mrs. Adenaka (Neighbor)

Minimum actors required: 5

## ACT I

The scene opens up inside BarStuck, a popular, trendy coffee shop in San Francisco, California. Two men, good friends and both residents of a nearby halfway house have just entered. Both men appear to be in their late-twenties to mid-thirties. One of the young men, Izzo, walks in a bold, confident manner, and is sporting a shaved head, jeans, T-shirt, and army jacket. His friend Spencer is a nervous, slight-built young man, wearing a button-down shirt and corduroy pants. He is struggling with an armful of envelopes and appearing uncomfortable with his surroundings.

Izzo: Grab us a table. I'll get the coffee. What do you want? House?

Spencer: Oh…uh, sure.

(Spencer, struggling to hold on to the envelopes, finally negotiates a seat and is staring out the window when Izzo returns, sloshing a trail of coffee behind him.)

Izzo: Here you go, dude.

(Izzo startles Spencer as he sets the cups and food down on the table. As Izzo pulls his chair out to sit down, he knocks the table behind him. There is a near miss as the young woman on the receiving end lunges to pull the book she is reading out of the path of her coffee that is now spilling from Izzo's impact. The young woman sighs loudly and shoots her best look of disgust in Izzo's direction. All of this is completely lost on Izzo as he directs his attention to the pile of mail Spencer has neatly stacked on the table.)

Izzo: Well, let's see what this week's bounty looks like.

(Izzo takes a large bite from a coffee-drenched croissant, wipes his hands on his pant legs and begins tearing open the envelopes Spencer has stacked on the table. From each one he extracts a letter of some sort that he folds into thirds and puts inside a manila envelope, and checks and cash, which he places inside a separate envelope. As he scans the notes he occasionally snorts or chortles before placing it inside the envelope. At one point, a letter causes Izzo to actually toss his head back in laughter.)

Spencer: Good news?

(Izzo grunts but does not answer. Several more seconds pass as he finishes going through the pile of mail and then shoves the envelopes with notes and money inside the pockets of his army jacket. He gathers the original envelopes and unwanted mail and stacks it on an empty chair. Izzo takes a big gulp of coffee, cocks his head for several seconds and stares out the window. )

Izzo: I've got to come up with another name. Something good…a woman's name…

        Lillith. No…Lila. Yeah, Lila…D'Vina. That's it. Lila D'Vina,

(Izzo sits silently for several seconds smiling and rubbing his chin.)

Spencer: So that is going to be the new name you are going to work under?

Izzo: (taking another gulp of coffee and then shaking his head) Nah. On second thought, it won't work. It conjures up images of some gypsy fortune-teller with a bandana around her head running her hands over a crystal ball.

(The woman at the next table rolls her eyes.)

Spencer: (surprised) *Gypsy?*

(Spencer shudders, take a drink of his coffee and then crosses his arms in front of his chest.)

Spencer: Did I ever tell you that I was scared to death of gypsies my entire childhood?

Izzo: (snorts) Why?

Spencer: Every time I did something wrong my mother would threaten to give me away to a band of gypsies. One time when I was still in kindergarten she actually put my coat and hat on me and packed my little suitcase. The whole time she was screaming that she was going to dump me off with the gypsies. She had all these horror stories about what they did to little kids. Man, I lived in fear of them.

(Spencer shakes his head and takes another drink of coffee. Izzo lets out a laugh.)

Izzo: Dude, your mother was a bitch.

(Spencer shudders and looks straight ahead as if he has not even heard Izzo.)

Spencer: (in a trance-like tone) One time, I think I was in second grade, this carnival came to town. My mother took me. There was this one guy with long black hair and a beard. His eyes were black too and really scary looking. He was dressed all in black and he had these long colored scarves hanging around his neck and a lot of jewelry on.

(Spencer pauses and stares into space as if calling in all of his memories.)

Spencer: Anyway, this guy had this sign that said, 'Psychic Cats' and these two weird-looking cats were sitting on this little podium. There was a white one and a black one. They had these little collars with fake jewels around their necks and these chains were attached to their collars. I'm pretty sure they were drugged.

Izzo: The Carnies?

Spencer: (chuckles) No, no, I mean the cats. I'm pretty sure of it.

Izzo: (snorts) Too much. So how were they supposed to be psychic?

Spencer: Oh…well…I'm not sure how people were supposed to think the cats were psychic. First you paid your money and picked either the white or the

|||
|---|---|
| | black cat, and then the guy held this open cigar box up to the cat you chose. The box was filled with these little rolled up papers with fortunes written on them. Anyway, the gypsy guy held up the box to the cat with one hand and in his other hand he held this little can of cat food right under the box. Then the cat would reach his paw towards the box and the guy would pick out a fortune near where the cat's paw had been. Then he would hand you your fortune. |
| Izzo: | (letting out a hearty laugh) That was it? That's how the cats were supposed to be psychic? |
| Spencer: | Yeah. That was all there was to it. |
| Izzo: | (still laughing) What a scam. |
| Spencer: | Well, the worst part was that my mother told me that she had already talked to the gypsies about me and she had brought me over there so they could see me. She said they were always looking for new kids and that they were real interested in taking me. |
| Izzo: | Ah, dude. That's cold. You're old lady is crazy, man, I'm telling you. |
| Spencer: | (hugging his body tightly) Anyway, for years after that I stayed up at night and peeked through the curtains watching for the band of gypsies that would be coming to get me. |

(The woman at the next table shifts in her chair and sneaks a glance over at Spencer.)

Spencer    :    (rocking back and forth gently in his seat, arms clutched tightly around his body)         I hate gypsies.

Izzo:         (grinning) Yeah, I'm sure you do.


(Several seconds pass. Izzo looks out the window. Spencer stares off into someplace all his own.)


Spencer:      (in a voice that was still hanging back somewhere in his own world) So we're going to get our own place this year, right?

Izzo:         Yeah. Sometime this year.

Spencer:      Izzo? It's definitely gonna' happen, right?

Izzo:         Yes. It's definitely going to happen. What choice do you have? You can't handle a place on your own when your time is up at the halfway house, and you sure as hell are not going back to live with that crazy old lady of yours.

Spencer:      I meant *you*. You're definitely gonna' do it, right?

Izzo:         Me? Live with your crazy old lady? I don't think so, dude. The goal is to try and stay *out* of prison. (laughs)

Spencer:      (worried tone) No, I meant you're still going to room with me in our own place, right?

Izzo:         (taking a rolled up napkin and throwing it at Spencer) I *know* what you meant. Lighten up, will you, Spence? We already talked about this.

(Spencer shifts in his seat and begins rocking again.)

Izzo: Ah, cut it out, Spence. All right. Yes. We are definitely getting our own place this year. Does that make you feel better? *Geezuz.* You're like a damned woman sometimes, I swear.

(The woman at the next table lets out a loud "tsk" sound and shakes her head. Izzo looks behind him at the woman. When she glances up at him he does not look away. Instead, he leans in closer to see what she is reading. Izzo looks at the front cover of the woman's book and then leans over to see the books on display in the middle aisle separating the tables from the front counter. Izzo snickers, gets up, and heads towards the book display marked, 'Oprah's Book Club: This month's selection.' He takes a copy of the book. As he heads back towards his table he looks around and notices for the first time that several people in the coffee shop are also reading the same book. A grin forms across his face as he returns to his table.)

Izzo: Hey Spence, Oprah personally recommends this.

(He announces this loudly, waving the book and then tossing it on to the table. Spencer grins and shifts in his chair in anticipation of what is to come.)

Well, now, let's see what makes this so special.

(He takes a seat and turns the book over and begins a dramatic reading of the back cover.)

'Laura *knows* what women want…an endless supply of chocolate and thin thighs.' (snorts) Apparently Laura doesn't understand the laws of physics.

All right. Let's see what other brilliant insights this Laura has.

(Spencer laughed and moves in closer)

Izzo: (loudly) 'She has only one dream…to finally discover a man who can give her what a box of Double Chocolate French Swirl Truffles does.' (snickers) What's that, exactly? A fat ass?

(Spencer laughs. The woman at the next table sighs loudly, gathers up her book and satchel and walks toward the door, stopping to give Izzo a dirty look on the way out. Izzo and Spencer laugh harder as the woman storms out of the coffee shop. Several people at nearby tables shake their heads or roll their eyes. Some whisper to one another as they look towards Izzo's table. Izzo looks around him and eyes each table slowly before turning back to Spencer.)

Izzo: (loudly) You know, Spence, that Oprah is really something. I think I feel inspired to write her a letter.

(Several people sneak glances towards Izzo. In high-drama fashion he digs a letter out of his pile of mail, turns the paper over and takes a pen from his jacket pocket to begin writing.)

Izzo: (loudly) OK. Let's see now. Where do we begin? She's done *so* much…

(rubs his chin and stares up toward the ceiling.)

Oh, oh, oh. Got it! Here goes… (begins writing)

'Dear Oprah,

I would like to let you know that your Angel Network show has inspired me to do something good for all of humanity. Therefore I am organizing a boycott of the Oprah Winfrey Show and the entire Oprah Book Club. I feel this will allow me to help those less fortunate than myself—individuals without the capacity to discern good taste or the wisdom and power to act in their own best interest. Your idea of helping people become "authenticated" amounts to helping them discover the importance of taking bubble-baths. Therefore, eliminating the Oprah Show (and your banal, insipid Book Club), I believe, will benefit all of humankind.

Thanks again for the inspiration,

*Yours truly,*

*A Real Life Angel*

P.S.—The so-called 'expert' guest you had on last week for the Fashion Make-Over Show who said (and I quote), "Pulling your hair back in to a pony-tail will give you an 'Instant High-Fashion Feel' is a real nitwit. She is exactly what I am talking about when I say it is in the best interest of the entire American public to have your show cancelled.'

(Spencer laughs hysterically, as he smacks the table repeatedly. Izzo, pleased with his performance, calmly folds the letter into thirds and carefully tucks it into his jacket pocket. For several seconds the coffee shop is filled with the sound of Spencer's howls. Izzo, grins and turns to look at the other customers. Several people look away, some begin whispering with one another. All of them have closed the books they were reading. The two men sit quietly for several seconds and then Izzo walks to the counter for two new cups of coffee and bagels.)

Izzo: (returns with the coffee and takes his seat) Oh, yeah. So, now what did you want to tell me earlier about some weirdness with a family that lives near the halfway house?

Spencer: (takes a sip of his new cup of coffee) Oh… I was talking to Peter Adenaka the other day and he told me this really weird story about his family.

Izzo: Who is he? Does he live on our block? I never heard of him.

Spencer: He and his parents live across the street from the halfway house. He has a little five-year old brother Bobby, too.

Izzo: Oh, you mean the people with the Buddha statue in their front lawn?

Spencer: (nodding) Yeah.

Izzo: The father…is he a quiet, mousy little guy?

Spencer: Yeah. That's Peter's dad. Anyway, I was talking with Peter the other day and get this…he's really bummed out because some kids he goes to school with saw him taking a leak and now they are teasing him and spreading rumors all over the school about him. He's really upset. He says if he were old enough, he would drop out.

Izzo: Just because someone saw him taking a whiz? What does he have…a miniature unit or something?

Spencer: No, no. It's nothing like that. It's that his mother makes him pee sitting down and…

Izzo: *What*? Are you kidding?

Spencer: Nope. She's been making him do it since the beginning.

Izzo: A real whack-job.

Spencer: Yeah. And listen to this…so Peter doesn't know any better because he's always been made to sit down. He never once has been able to stand up while he pees so…

Izzo: Wait a minute. How does his mother know what he does when he is in the bathroom?

Spencer: She watches him. She's like a clean-freak or something and she makes him keep the door open so she can watch to make sure he doesn't ever leave a mess.

Izzo: (groans and shakes his head) *Geezuz*.

Spencer: Anyway, so he was peeing sitting down in the locker room and some kids he goes to school with saw him.

Izzo: How?

Spencer: I think they were standing on something looking over the stall. Anyway, now they are teasing him real bad and there are all these rumors going around. The things they are saying about him are brutal. He is really depressed. I swear he seems like he may be suicidal.

(Izzo shakes his head in disgust)

Izzo: Wait a minute…what about his father? Where is *he* when all this is going on?

Spencer: Oh, he has to pee sitting down, too.

Izzo: *What?* (groans loudly)

Spencer: Yeah…Peter's mother makes her husband keep the door open when he goes to the bathroom, too. She actually stands there and watches him. Peter said so. But, anyway, to answer your question, his dad isn't really going to be able to do anything to help Peter.

Izzo: (shaking his head) If it is the same family I am thinking of, I've already had a few choice words for that woman. She was out there a couple weeks ago slapping the younger kid around, making him do some weird cleansing routine. I hate those damned clean-freaks. Disease, my ass. OCD. (shakes head) Damned narcissists is what they are. They think they are so special that the rest of the world is going to contaminate them.

(Spencer sighs and takes a gulp of his coffee)

Izzo: So the house this woman lives in…it's definitely the yellow one with the Buddha statue, right?

Spencer: Yeah. That's the one. They just put that Buddha out there a few months ago.

Izzo: Well, I guess this woman has a completely different definition of what Buddha stands for than what I've read.

(Izzo snorts and shakes his head again. The two men remain silent for a couple seconds, as if trying to make sense of it all. Suddenly Izzo looks at his watch.)

Izzo: C'mon, Spence. We've got to head back.

Spencer: (looking at his own watch) It's 5:15! We're gonna' be late for kitchen duty. Marna is going to kill us!

Izzo: Relax, Spence. Marna is House Manager, not God.

(Izzo gathers up the envelopes and the empty coffee cups and dumps all of them into the trashcan. Then he reaches into his jacket pocket and pulls out the envelope filled with cash and checks.)

Izzo: I've got to make a slight detour. You go on ahead. And, give this envelope to Mrs. F. No doubt she has done the books today and is probably at her wit's end by now. (hands Spencer the envelope) Just tell her that I had a much better month than expected and to put the extra toward the new hot water heater.

Spencer: (confused) Oh, uh...OK.

Izzo: All right. You better pick up the pace, dude. See you back at the house.

Spencer: Are you sure?

Izzo: Yeah. Listen, when you get in, tell Marna I'm there. Just say I'm right outside. Tell her I'm checking on the water for the cats and I'll be right in. (Spencer nods)

All right. Go on.

(The stage lights go out. When the lights return, Izzo is leaning against a fence post and smoking a cigarette. After only one drag from the cigarette the tranquility is broken by yelling coming from across the street. The backside of an overweight woman can be seen moving towards a Buddha lawn statue. Though he is blocked by the woman and cannot be seen, a small child can be heard.)

Mrs. Adenaka: Dust yourself off, you idiot! *Now*! Just do it or I'll do it *for* you!

(The woman doing the screaming is yanking a small child around by his hair. Though the child remains blocked from view, she maneuvers the child in front of the fountain lawn statue of Buddha. Izzo steps a couple of feet over to get a better look. He takes another drag off his cigarette, inhales and exhales slowly as he watches. His left hand clinches tightly then relaxes.)

Mrs. Adenaka: Harder, god-damnit! Your face, idiot. Don't forget your face...*Forget it*. I guess I'm going to have to do it for you. Get over here!
(There are sounds of a small boy sobbing.)

Mrs. Adenaka: Stop your blubbering! (there are slapping sounds as the woman moves her hands roughly over and over the child's face.) Whose fault is it anyway? Huh? Huh? Answer me!

(There are sounds of the boy crying harder)

Mrs. Adenaka: Shut up. This is your own doing. I warned you to stay away from him. I warned you!

(The woman begins frantically hitting at the child's shirt and pants as if beating off some imaginary leeches. The boy continues to sob. The woman brings her arm back and swats the child across the side of the head, causing him to lose his balance and stumble forward. The sounds of a child screaming can be heard.)

Mrs. Adenaka: Shut up!

Izzo: (throws his cigarette to the ground) Hey, you crazy bitch! How'd you like it if I came over there and smacked *you* around?

Mrs. Adenaka: (looking up surprised) Why don't you mind your own fucking business?

Izzo: Child abuse *is* my business, you lard-ass bitch. You better leave that kid alone or I'll get the cops over here.

Mrs. Adenaka: (turning her attention back to the boy) Get in the house! Now!

(turning back in Izzo's direction) God-damned crazy neighbors have nothing better to do except butt in to other people's business, I guess. Moron halfway-house losers! It is bad enough they are bringing all of our property values down. Imagine… bottom-feeders who cannot even function in society, who think they can tell me how to treat my own child!

(There are sounds of the child, whimpering. The woman moves away from the statue and heads toward her house.)

Izzo: Hey, you…Elephant-ass…You better keep your hands off that kid. I'm watching you!

(There is the sound of a slamming door. Izzo shakes his head and turns to walk back to the halfway-house. As he approaches the door, he is met by Spencer.)

Spencer: Oh, Izzo, Mrs. F. said to tell you that you are an angel sent from heaven…and, um, oh yeah…she says she doesn't know how she can ever repay you.

Izzo: All right, thanks for giving me the message, man.

(Spencer nods and walks away)

The stage lights go out.

A clock strikes midnight. A dim light reveals Izzo and Spencer are outside smoking cigarettes. A full moon is casting an eerie mixture of light and fog giving off a false sense of purity. The two of them stand together on the sidewalk for several minutes, silent, except for the sounds of their inhaling and exhaling.)

Izzo: C'mon. (he motions; his voice startles Spencer)

Spencer: Where are we going? (shifts uncomfortably)

(Izzo points across the street towards the yellow house.)

Izzo: To Bitch Adenaka's Buddha.

Spencer: What are we going to do? (Spencer is visibly excited)

Izzo : (snorts) I've got a special prayer I need answered.

(The stage lights go out again. There are mysterious, muffled sounds. Next, a dim light reveals the silhouettes of the two men slipping unnoticed past the houses on their return to the halfway house. Izzo, smirking, shoulders back, moves his broad frame swiftly but quietly down the sidewalk. Spencer half walks, half runs on tiptoe a couple of feet behind. He stops every few seconds and bends over in half with laughter.)

Spencer: Man, where did you *get* that?" (laughs)

Izzo: *Sshhh*. Just come on.

Spencer: Did you get that from Marna's room?...Izzo?...Izzo, did you take that from Marna's room?

(Izzo keeps walking in silence. Suddenly, he comes to an abrupt stop, turns and looks back. The clouds have passed and the moonlight is now shining and reflecting brightly on the Great One. Izzo smiles.)

Izzo: Buddha in weeds. Buddha with dribbling fountain. Buddha, the Keeper of the Curb. Buddha grinning…with a flaming red strap-on erection.

(Silence. The lights go dark on the actors and remains only on Buddha. The curtain closes.)

**The End**

# GROUNDED
## A
## SHORT PLAY

by
LEE GOODEN

CHARACTERS
CA-CAPTAIN ADAM
CB-CAPTAIN BRUCE

SCENE: An airport bar. CA and CB are two off-duty pilots sitting a table. CB is drinking excessively from a shot glass that he continually fills from a large liquor bottle, CA is nursing a glass of water.

CA: I can fly.

CB: (drinks) And that is why we have thousands of hours logged with this air line.

CA: I'm not talking about flying in a plane.

CB: (shakes his head) Ok then. I've got the red eye tomorrow night. (drinks) You'd better get some rest, you're going back on duty tonight and you sound tired, you're not making much sense (drinks).

CA: I'm never tired of flying.
(pause)

CB: (drinks)Yeah, well I get tired of the politics, gonna say the hell with this commercial crap and start flying private or find me a governmental gig (drinks)…you should check that out too…great money and good bennies (drinks).

CA: I've got wings.

CB: Pilots brother, we're a special breed (drinks).

CA: I want to soar.

CB: Nothing like it in the world…nothing like it…let's make a toast to pilots.
(they toast CB drinks a double shot)

(pause)

CA: My shoulder blades are hollow.

CB: (drinks) Ouch! Painful! Sounds genetic.

CA: They are confined and compartmentalized.

CB: Your shoulders?

CA: My wings…they're compressed into my shoulder blades

CB: You could pin them to your jacket like everybody else.

CA: They will unfurl and I will glide along the moonbeams

CB: We should know better than to drink so much before a job.

CA: I'm not drinking, but I'm drunk with flight.

CB: I'll drink to that! (has 3-4 shots in a row) I hear ya…(sings off-key) Fly like an eagle, up, up, and away…leaving on a jet plan…would you like to swing on a star, fly me to the moon…come fly with me, come fly with me…I believe I can fly, I believe I can touch the sky. WHAT a rush!

CA: God gave me my wings.

CB: (drinks) I'm so high and so fast that I can't catch my breath. I'm so high, I can't catch myself. The hell with God.

CA: I can fly.

CB: I know.

CA: I've got wings, but we're grounded, you're grounded.

CB: I know

CA: You're grounded and I'm fallen.

(lights dim)

end

(C) Lee Gooden 2006, 2007

# WILLIAM SHAKENBEER

**A Play By**

Daniel Scott
Batten

DEDICATED TO:

William Shakespeare

**©Daniel Scott Batten,
2007**

## DRAMATIS PERSONAE
### (CHARACTERS OF THE PLAY)

Shakenbeer
Young Boy
Sir-Reverence Puddingprick
Random Poor Lady
Shakenbeer's Dead Conscience
Wealthy Man
Haggard Old Lady
Hamlet
Lady Mopealot
Batten (As Creator)

## SCENE ONE

## ACT ONE

Play opens in the slums of London in 1603. Shakenbeer is walking and meets a boy on the street that he wishes to teach the ways of learning, wit and eloquence.

SHAKENBEER – Boy, come here and stand next to your father. For I shall prove to thee a most prominent and powerful friend. Come and I shall aid you in the **sheer of shield**[xii] found in words **well seen.**[xiii]

YOUNG BOY – I am **artless**, Sir, make me most **artful**![xiv]

[Putting his arm around the boy and bringing him close and looking down upon him with affection says…]

SHAKENBEER – In approach of art and all the grandest of dreams one must gleam their prideful jewels beneath the golden **arch**[xv] of great **aspect**[xvi] and not be afraid to be a mere **apron-man**[xvii] of his thoughts. Let the words make of you, and not you make them,

[Looking up with puppy eyes the boy admires his new teacher and emboldened by the influence of his wisdom, starts skipping and twirling his arms, breaking loose from his master and singing 'Lo, the wantonesse be gone and mere dreams are coins cashed now here in this heaven…' and then he tripped on his own feet and then fell in the open sewer, covering himself in filth to the amusement of the other poor peoples about the street.]

RANDOM POOR LADY- Aye, look and take yer lesson, don't go chasing dreams when you are no better then shit. Shit cannot aspire to be, but a bigger shit. See this boy, see how he is shit, trying to be a Gentleman. And a boy too!

[Pointing to the old and poor woman Shakenbeer says]

SHAKENBEER – Woman! Have mercy on the child. Your pollution snares entirely too many noses roundabout this pathetic towne. I know this entirely too seriously, and here you make your prey but a boy, you **boy-queller**,[xviii] I ought to, if I was less a Christian, have you greeted by the charges of witchery!

RANDOM POOR LADY – Lo! Kill this!

[She spat a big old goober and it landed right on Shakenbeer's face, and slowly dripped upon his chest until the awesome ball of flem landed at his feet to the earth-shaking laughter of the poor wretches that witnessed the whole thing.]

Now! Go and write that in one of your plays about the tragic flaw in being spat upon by a wretch as vile and evil as I. You can call it 'Lady-Vile That Damned Boy-Queller.'

[The crowd ate this up and laughed so hard soon the lot of them were on the ground boiling in aching laughter at Shakenbeer's expense.]

SHAKENBEER'S DEAD CONSCIENCE (just a voice) – Hummingbird, oh how hummingbird pooh is the guise of the fool.[xix]

[Shakenbeer puts his finger to his lips and says hush to the invisible specter that stands at his side (i.e. his dead conscious) and looking to distract the boy from his craziness points to a friend he finds in the crowd and says:]

SHAKENBEER- Lo! Look! There is **Sir-Reverence Puddingprick!**[xx] My most esteemed fan and hysterical engineer of my fame.

[He points wildly at a man well dressed for the day who whistled as he counted thus…]

SIR-REVERENCE PUDDINGPRICK- One, two, three, four, five, six, …

SHAKENBEER-Puddingprick!
Sir Puddingprick! Come and join this mere boy and me in the great philosophical powers of **breathing**.[xxi] Why do you count so?

PUDDINGPRICK – Happily I shall make whatever goodness I have the **brawn**[xxii] that we shall all **bring out**[xxiii] into one as powerful as Briareus.[xxiv] I count so because thus rids a man of his warts. See [he points to his nose] there be seven devils about me nose.

SHAKENBEER'S DEAD CONSCIENCE – I know hummingbird pooh when I see it, and smell it, and taste it, and…

SHAKENBEER- SHUT UP! Indeed life is hard enough without you, must you torment me or shall I kill thee again?

PUDDINGPRICK – Sir!! How dare you say such **soore**[xxv] and **vein may bane**[xxvi] be words to a friend, a lover and me?

[Cutting off his own voice before it exposes his true idiocy, points to a young boy in the crowd that is dressed in soiled clothing whilst trying to appear an aristocrat...]

SHAKENBEER – Look there at that soiled-mess of man vying to be a Sir, wearing those vulgar **broques**[xxvii] he stole off some minor shoe –keeper!

[The lot of them laughed, laughed it good, in fact too good that a button off Sir-Reverence Pudding pricks fancy coat went flying and hit a wealthy man in the eye.]

[The wealthy man looks around trying to find the culprit of such crime that had his eye watering and his makeup running...]

WEALTHY MAN – Scoundrels! Bloody no-good-for-nothing scoundrels! I shall find who is responsible for this defamation, and when I do, that person shall meet the rope!

[Disgusted the snob of a man walks away waving his hands in the air wildly and cursing out obscenities as he pushes his way through the busy streets.]

SHAKENBEER – I am afraid we have gotten off treacherously. Let us begin again my dear wretch. **In a line**[xxviii] my better senses **gree thee sty above the Zoilus**[xxix] and strive more to **blast ye trumpets** and to **blazen Oaten reeds!**[xxx] Now son, what think ye of this?

YOUNG BOY – I shall **reed Phœbus**[xxxi] from your example and **parbreake my maw and gorge the clownish trespass**[xxxii] so I might clear my throat and compel your words to live inside of me.

SHAKENBEER – **Armed to point,**[xxxiii] **my later** genius,[xxxiv] I shall embark to make you **speak frogs**[xxxv] from out of your mouth and learn the guise of making fools more foolish as to say completely nothing so that the idiot might become your admirer. There are few intellects, and yeah, so many idiots, your legions shall be bigger if you traduce the idiot into loving your eloquent babble. Like me, consider the **vnkindly imps**[xxxvi] who wash my feet and bade I kiss their daughters so they might break my heart and convince me to write an immortal poem in their names.

[Shakenbeer then leads them to three haggard ladies who are emptying their chamber pots in the gutter beside the road and interrupts their singing...and speaking to the most lovely of the three who stands in the middle..]

SHAKENBEER- Dear ladies I am The Writer, Wimpy Wane Shakenbeer. I **gan espye**[xxxvii] of your handsome daughters and wondered, **wher seystow**,[xxxviii] I write them a poem and **hevenisshly**[xxxix] put their beauty in my quill and write their names in the mind of every single courtier from here to France!

HAGGARD LADY – I am not sure I have heard of you. Sir, for all I know you are a **forpined clarrce, dreadful celle fantastic**! Pray this, tell me, **at the leeste weye**[xl] **by vein imaginacioun,**[xli] something you hath scribbled so I may make good judge of your character.

SHAKENBEER – My Good Lady, I wrote the play about two torn lovers who vyed by affection to spite the **despitously**[xlii] opposing families and the gentleman went to the window in winter, struck, **cridestow**,[xliii] for his lover to take his rose. It was called "A Roman and his Jewel All Wet."

HAGGARD LADY – I will it to you that you may gaze the lushus prize and make print of her eyes, no thighs to be unlaced, and **youre plesaunce**[xliv], leave you to **brenningly**[xlv] give praise to my joy.

[She turns and walks in and calls with a wretched voice to her daughter]

Hamlet! Come out, let a poet gander upon your lush bosom, and give esteem to thee by praise in print to be!

HAMLET – Here **I pluck up my plausive flesh**[xlvi] so you may make **plain-songs**[xlvii] heavenly throngs!

SHAKENBEER – Reeling-ripe, my eyes, my heart sings this religious tune – Hamlet reprehend my reproach, for I report the beauty that spills from your soul infects and ravels me sore. Sore your lips, my lips wish to sip such remorseful a rose, as Hamlet! O Hamlet I want, but cannot, for forbidden fruits are sweeter, to pluck thy rose and feed thee by the ambrosia of the man-quill.

YOUNG BOY – Compelled by such moving prose, I feel my head revolting against the normalcy of my upbringing and I fear I may fall over in awe.

PUDDINGPRICK – Pray hear this, when you feel a vulgar pulse in the head, and ache thus, I appease you to try my remedy. If all this **caret tempus non habes moribus**[lxlviii] moves your mind to pains, then I advise you take a page from Shakenbeer's *Nothing To Do About Doing Nothing*, and after **crying over a corpse**[xlix] and dipping the page in the tears, wrap the paper about your head for three minutes before you come clean of the unseemliness of sorrow.

---
l

[At this Hamlet lifts her blouse and shows that she indeed is a man to which Shakenbeer cries...]

SHAKENBEER – I shall write a play of such treachery! I shall call it Hamlet and wherever you go from hence you shall be shamed and guilted by this offense. Publish this I will, and I will make my coin from the destitute mouths so hungry with such tasty gossip!

## ACT TWO

Following a few minutes of silence to appease the wrathful anger of the enraged and thinking Shakenbeer they walk until he shouts out victorious!

SHAKENBEER – I have it now! A great poem of love and pornography! It shall begin thus:

Pardon, sweet flower of matchless poetry,
And fairest bud the red rose ever bare,
Although my muse divorc'd from deeper care
Presents thee with a wanton elegy...

[Interrupting Shakenbeer is his moment of idiocy..]

YOUNG BOY – My Dear Sir, that is the poetry of one Thomas Nashe, and it is from his wild poem about a dildo called, *A Choice of Valentines*.

SHAKENBEER – Sure? How could such brilliance come but by the lantern of another? Is it possible someone has beaten me to this?

SHAKENBEER'S DEAD CONSCIOUS – That bloat stole it from thee Sir, after all things of shit are a species of feces.

SHAKENBEER- Give me my scallop-shell of quiet, my staff of faith to walk upon, my scrip of joy, immortal diet, my bottle of salvation, my gown of glory, hope's true gage, and thus I'll take my pilgrimage...[1]

PUDDINGPRICK – So **dearly designed**,[li] such rich and true eloquence, sir. The best poem I think you have ever recited to me of your great list of works. Indeed!

YOUNG BOY – Again, I apologize to correct you both, but indeed that is a Sir Raleigh poem, A brave man indeed is he.

[They are interrupted by a funeral party who are carrying a coffin out of a hobble and behind them the mourning widow wipes the threshold clean]

PUDDINGPRICK – Let us follow that procession and see if we cannot dig the fresh corpse up and **poure**[lii] over the corpse **for eyes and hand.**[liii] You sir, my favorite and most pretty poet may make a sweet sonnet of such morbid occasion. You can bring the world to such heights of fatality and make pun on that old and ancient saying, "Drink and be merry for tomorrow ye shall surely die."

SHAKENBEER- I shall **brain**[liv] me a golden sonnet and give mark to the man and I shall **be with…to bring!**[lv]

YOUNG BOY – Don't go **pissing water before tossing your nets,**[lvi] Sir. Indeed you are a brilliant calibre, but a **calibre**[lvii] only can you be. Give the world joy, and stretch your handsome frames about the average opinion, ye, but do not pretend to be God himself and all that you do be so fabulous and rich. Or else indeed, it shall be fabulous, and as lies attract more lies, you will have a beast to tame, a beast of your own mistruths. A billion men hath fallen to their own creatures.

SHAKENBEER- (Laughing, bemused) Am I **boring**[lviii] you, child, with my rhetoric? (Rubbing his head until the child's cap falls off) If I take myself too serious I tell you to write a play thyself and make me **boy my greatness**[lix] there upon the handsome stage.

PUDDINGPRICK – (Now the lot of them are skipping and laughing) **Two men pissing ends in war,**[lx] what about three!! (The three fall upon the ground, tripping on their gaiety and suddenly after a few minutes of frolicking, Sir Puddingprick says…) LOOK! They are walking **across a field! With the coffin!**[lxi] We must not follow, or we shall be as barren as now the future is for that field there!

SHAKENBEER- Hey! Look yonder it is Lady Mopealot and it appears she is selling cakes. It seems like some kind of madness has happened in towne - witches must be back! Let us go see!

LADY MOPEALOT- Get your cakes! Fed them to whomever you need fend off or whomsoever you need cast back to hell with the eyes of evil. Get your Witches cakes! Get your witches Cakes! Get 'em here!

PUDDINGPRICK – Hello my **maid-pale malmsey-nosed**[lxii] friend! I do love your bakeries. Is it **Urine cakes**[lxiii] then?

LADY MOPEALOT- Indeed it is, a favorite of yours is it? (The Two laugh)

YOUNG BOY- Look those who have bought them knew not their purpose, and look how they react!

[There is a crowd of purchasers who ate the cakes themselves and are puking all around them and up the streets.]

LADY MOPEALOT- Well then, we know there is no witch in them then! They ate the cakes of their own free will no witch would do that. Such is our luck (They continue chuckling). Why not come into my abode for some **language**[lxiv] and **inch-thick ridiculousness!**[lxv]

PUDDINGPRICK – Sounds clever! Let us be gay!

## ACT THREE

[They follow Lady Mopealot into her house and duck at the low ceiling. She leads them to sit down and she gathers a basket of dry bread, old cheese and puts them on the table.

She then gets a pitcher of homemade ale, and makes available some cigars.]

PUDDINGPRICK – Cynthia! Lo Cynthia, how brightly you have cast your beams upon us with all these offerings, offerings given from such pure heart to a bunch of **deboshed, daff and corky**[lxvi] souls! You certainly are of a sweeter cake then us. (He raises his fresh poured mug of beer in the air and after nodding three times to her, sips it.)

SHAKENBEER – Praises be! Indeed, we are blessed today (he also raises his beer and takes a healthy swig)

YOUNG BOY – The cheese and the bread, It has been weeks since I have had the pleasure of so much food before me! (He cuts a piece of cheese and raises it, nods three times at her and partakes).

LADY MOPEALOT- Pride praises the explosion,[lxvii] So if you don't mind, be weary of puking such boasts for I have no good mop to clean up the mess!
SHAKENBEER- A Woman with a bit of spit and salt! Praise be to a woman with a tongue as sharp and pristine as the blade on that one! (He picks up his cigar and lights it from the candle burning in the middle of the table).

PUDDINGPRICK – Never more dangerous is a woman with a crumb of wit! (He chuckles to himself)

LADY MOPEALOT- A bit of **cow dung in that mouth**[lxviii] of yours might just get that vulgarity out. Certainly, you are infected by some witch to say such brave words in so cowardly a fashion, and in the presence of a Lady at that! (She laughs wildly).

YOUNG BOY – Have you any butter for thee bread, dear Lady?

LADY MOPEALOT – If ye wish to find some butter here in London I know a goodly witch who brews it in her caldron and **stirs it with a dead man's hand,**[lxix] and never is it so smooth or creamy. Go now and run three houses up if you wish for butter! She is good enough not to turn you into a frog. (The whole of the room laughs, and the young boy's face turns red with embarrassment and he sinks in his seat until his eyes are barely visible over the rim of the table.)

SHAKENBEER – (Rubbing the child's head) **all well is weal, all death is to please.**[lxx] Rise up child; be not afraid, no witches can find us so long as we have the worst of them here in our friendship. (They all laugh, and the kid soon rises to join in the laughter.)

PUDDINGPRICK – Standup all, and let us sing the praise of cheap beer, cheap cigars and cheap friends! (They all stand and give a mock cheer and sing 'Hip Hip Hooray' three times over before returning to their seats).

SHAKENBEER- (Look over at Mopealot) **A Ball less waste is what you are!**[lxxi] (Mopealot slaps him hard)

LADY MOPEALOT – To say such a thing! How dare you?

SHAKENBEER- It is not my fault it is written in the script. (Pulling a booklet out of his coat pocket, he places it on the table, opens it to the dialogue of current reference and)

See, it is right here! I am to say, 'A ball less waste is what you are! (Indigent she tosses her hands in the air and curses)

LADY MOPEALOT – It is bad enough he named me so poorly! Lady MOPE-A LOT! Now he, my creator, that vile and arrogant prick of a Batten never so **batten,**[lxxii] calls me a ball less waste!

SHAKENBEER – Maybe indeed he is **batten**,[lxxiii] all to batten. So Batten he is unhealthy.

YOUNG BOY – I think our creator just expresses what he desires of us, a sense of humor, After all he is aware of our mockery of him before we are, and still allows it! Indeed, the joke is on us all. And at his expense too!

PUDDINGPRICK – He has most certainly made ye wise, wise beyond us all in this meager thing called intellect!

SHAKENBEER – It is for us to enjoy, and on his coin too. He loves us so that he gives us importance, and indeed, He gives us the chance to revel in our own fealty. I am moved to tears, tears of joy. (At this he gets up and raises his mug of beer and starts to utter a cheer when he looses handle on it and drops it on the table and loosing his footing he falls back in his chair, which then breaks the chair at the vulgar amusement of his friends)

LADY MOPEALOT – Indeed! Our creator gleefully laughs and means no wretchedness. Look, his jokes never cease to amaze. Nor cease to injure.

SHAKENBEER – (Slamming his fists down on the table and angrily yelling) Why me? Why must I be the butt of all his joking?

PUDDINGPRICK – **All wet with questions**[lxxiv] are you? The great imponderable questions of life! Why? Why indeed.

YOUNG BOY – Indeed not! Not why? But Why not! Is not this horror **enclaved in our ears, the reins and the whips for all manner of madness that in association with its torture is the source of all that is pleasure?**[lxxv] Certainly, you are no ape called Evolution, even if you rode **Batten's axle.** [lxxvi]

PUDDINGPRICK- Perchance, Batten might have his master also! Perchance he is but a man, a man that is a God in this realm, but in the realm of realms, in that ultimate realm he is just a man who is mastered by his own chains, and his own desires!

YOUNG BOY – Yes! Yes you have gotten it!

SHAKENBEER – So are we just vehicles of his vanity? Are we expressions of his own desire to be more than just a man in a realm where his kind of manliness is not more vivid or important as ours? (Curious he now looks down upon the manuscript and upon turning the pages he finds that someone is to betray him and is meant to kill him)

It seems as my master wishes, or rather, that he warns me that one of you, the evil one, shall betray me by the garden in the center of towne. Upon his commandment, I am to go meet my doom!

## SCENE TWO

SHAKENBEER – Batten! Why must art repel its artist? Why must our children turn against us? For what reason am I to be the target of thy wrath? Why do you mock me so, by giving me this chance at life to take it away so? Is not Art our mutual master? Or is the lesson that art is our mutual monster? Why must art when all is said and done, be artless?

BATTEN – (A voice only) I mock you not Sir! I mock your reputation. I mock the foolishness that is art to those who gaze upon the tool, the experience that is art, with such contempt. I mock those who draw unloved conclusions, who make heroes of our insanity and put on the masks of us, thinking themselves equals with that divine force that enabled them to know such greatness. I mock not Shakespeare; I mock those idiots who mock art, by measuring art by such silly measures. No mere man can be divine, and no lesson is superior to alternate lessons. Behold the greatest joke, the joke that is the thought that the world might know heaven by repelling it. God saves all, all who drop this world, and come out of the illusion that are held in these pages, and are held here in my mind. I too must drop the illusion of the pages I fill, and look not to the pages themselves, but to He that hath rendered them and ask Him, to let me transcend the ink that invented me!

[Entering from off stage left is the Young Boy who creeps wielding a dagger. He creeps up to the kneeling Shakenbeer and plunges the dagger into his back, killing him...]

## **FINIS**

Join Read Herrings Journal at

Myspace.com/Readherringsjournal

Or send submissions for future editions to

Readherringsjournal@writeme.com

# ENDNOTES

[i] Phrase was once used to describe vessels in transit

[ii] [Latin] Not currently existing but ready to come into existence under certain conditions in the future.

[iii] [Latin] Going, remaining, and returning. This phrase was once used to describe a person who is privileged from arrest while traveling to the place where assigned duties are to be performed, while remaining there, and while returning. *Blacks Law Dictionary, 2005.*

[iv] Smiths or those who work with fire to forge iron that are helots (or slaves) to the conformity of the product.

[v] Possession in the Christian Soteriology, or the cooperation within consciousness of free will and divine grace in the process of conversation and regeneration

[vi] (Latin) 'Against the world.'

[vii] Horace 65-8 BCE, *Odes*, II, ii 6-7, (Adapted by Michel de Montaigne).

[viii] Latin for 'Of Cambridge [University]'.

[ix] Seneca, *Epistle. Moral.*, LIX15

[x] Oxford University slang for a fellow worthy of talking too.

[xi] Losers/frustrated youths. The pun falls upon the phrase 'close but no cigar' which originated from old time fairs. Men would be given an extraordinarily hard task such as hold a heavy hammer and swing it with so great force it hit the bell that was suspended a distance above them, and etc. and the concessionaire encouraged boys and men to further efforts by giving them a nickel. Saying, "Close – but no cigar!'

[xii] (Shakespearean) Nothing but a defense

[xiii] (Shakespearean) well-skilled i.e. words well chosen and backed by great understanding prove to be most valuable weapons.

[xiv] (Shakespearean) Artless = unskilled and artist/artful = Scholar

[xv] (Shakespearean) Chief master [God]

[xvi] (Shakespearean) Influence attributed to the positions of the heavenly bodies. [I.e the heavens]

[xvii] (Shakespearean) Mechanic

[xviii] (Shakespearean) Boy-killer

[xix] Supposed to be nonsense, as clearly it is…

[xx] Sir-reverence = Shakespeare's corruption of 'save-reverence' or An apologetic response PUDDINGPRICK =(Thomas Nashe 1567-1601? Used this work in his *Pierce Penniless [1592]*) and it Means "Skewer"

[xxi] (Shakespearean) Language (of poetry and philosophy)

[xxii] (Shakespearean) Fleshy mass of the body

[xxiii] (Shakespearean) give birth to

[xxiv] A giant with a hundred hands

[xxv] (Shakespearean) Severely (meant words)
[xxvi] (Shakespearean) Deluded words and death wishing words
[xxvii] (Shakespearean) Rude kind of shoe, generally, made of untamed hide.
[xxviii] (Shakespearean) On a lead
[xxix] (Shakespearean) Favour that you ascend the bitter critics (such as Zoilus who was a severe critic of Homer and thus his name is synonymous with a carping critic.)
[xxx] (Shakespearean) Speak heroic poetry and give due praise to pastoral poems
[xxxi] (Shakespearean) See the sun (i.e. the 'light' in eloquence
[xxxii] (Shakespearean) Vomit my stomach and [clean my] throat [of] the rustic sin (rustic sin = the average ignorance of good language and art.)
[xxxiii] (Shakespearean) Fully armed
[xxxiv] (Shakespearean) My most recent student
[xxxv] [Revelations 16:13 'And I saw three unclean spirits like frogs come out of the mouth of the dragon, and out of the beast, and out of the mouth of the false prophet! Also see Exodus 8:2-7]
[xxxvi] (Shakespearean) Unnatural Children (i.e. the poor and ungentle)
[xxxvii] (Shakespearean) Caught site of
[xxxviii] (Shakespearean) do you say this (bid me permission)
[xxxix] (Shakespearean) In a heavenly manner
[xl] (Shakespearean) at least
[xli] (Shakespearean) deluded assumption (of being a proper writer)
[xlii] (Shakespearean) Angrily
[xliii] Did cry out
[xliv] To please you
[xlv] (Shakespearean) Burningly
[xlvi] (Shakespearean) I give myself to thee to rouse thee with my pleasing
[xlvii] (Shakespearean) Simple melodies
[xlviii] (Thomas Nashe 1567-1601?) Meaning is unknown (Probably meant to mean nonsense)
[xlix] (Superstition) "If you allow your tears to fall on the dead, they will have no rest." [M. TREVELYAN *Folk-Lore of Wales* 283 (1909)].
[l] From Sir Walter Raleigh, 1554?-1618, *The Passionate Man's Pilgrimage*
[li] (Shakespeare) Richly put into view
[lii] (Shakespearean) Look closely; gaze
[liii] …**for eyes**… Superstition says that it be a good sign if the eyes of the said corpse do not shut themselves…**and hand**…AD 77 *Natural History XXVII xi* Scofula..and throat diseases..may be cured by the contact of the hand of a person who has been carried off by an early death…
[liv] (Shakespearean) Conceive in the mind
[lv] (Shakespearean) Upper hand of (be given the upper hand of fame)
[lvi] In Folklore and superstition a sailor if he pissed over the side of the boat before the nets were cast, they ship would have to return to the port and start again another day.
[lvii] (Shakespearean) a pun on bore, a small caliber or whole.
[lviii] (Shakespearean) Another pun on bore (small hole) but meant as a jab at "boring" the kid i.e. annoying….

[lix] (Shakespearean) Boys took female parts on the Elizabethan stage.
[lx] " "Tis an old received opinion, that if two doe pee together they shall quarrel." –John Aubrey *Remaines of Gentillisme and Judaisme* 1686-88
[lxi] The superstition goes, that if a coffin is carried across a field it shall be barren thereafter.
[lxii] (Shakespearean) White-complexioned, red-nosed
[lxiii] 'Another to bring in the witch.' To house the hag, you must doe this; commix with meale a little Pisse of him bewicht; then forthwith make a little wafer of a cake: And this rawly bak't will bring the Old Hag in. –Robert Herrick *Hesperides* 336. (1648)
[lxiv] (Shakespearean) Power of speech
[lxv] (Shakespearean) Solid silliness that is beyond all doubt
[lxvi] (Shakespearean) Debauched, put off and withered...
[lxvii] From the root explōdere or, "to drive out by clapping."
[lxviii] Such was the superstition that cow dung placed in a cow's mouth would prevent theft and keep witches and fairies away.
[lxix] Superstition says this is a good way to get some creamy smooth butter, NO KIDDING!
[lxx] All that is well is a lesion; all pain brings pleasure in living.
[lxxi] No man are you and so you are a waste of wit (Waste = empty. The pun is on the root Vāstus)
[lxxii] Secure
[lxxiii] Fat (Batten = "to fatten" and "Secure" among other definitions)
[lxxiv] A little old pun of mine on the root of WHAT = Wet (The Old Frisian form of the root for the modern 'what')
[lxxv] A pun on Enclave, "surrounded by land owned by someone else" [1435] In this case it is being surrounded by a noise, a noise they cannot own and cannot dismiss. All music is just noise that we accept as music, hence, if you listen closely to the noise, you shall find some music in it.
[lxxvi] You shall not grasp Batten even if you should ride his back (i.e. the axis of his creation). For his creation is too far beyond us, that if he should tell us we would still not understand, what and why.

www.ingramcontent.com/pod-product-compliance
Ingram Content Group UK Ltd.
Pitfield, Milton Keynes, MK11 3LW, UK
UKHW051254180426
11947UKWH00020B/1716